You're not broken.
You just haven't found what brings you to life yet...

SECRET OF THE BROKEN KING

THE POSEIDON TRIALS

ELIZA RAINE

ROSE WILSON

CHAPTER 1

*N*ever underestimate a librarian.

My lungs burned. My feet pounded the wooden flooring, but I could see the massive ornate doors looming closer. I willed my muscles to hold out, pushing through the pain and racing through the museum hall toward the stairwell that led up and out to freedom.

"Stop! Come back here!"

I had thought I was lucky that the archives in the museum didn't have security guards. Little did I know that they didn't need them - because the librarians were built like frigging Olympic athletes. If I wasn't desperately trying to escape with the ten-pound book I'd stolen, I might have taken some time to admire the biceps of the guy chasing me. As it was, I kept my focus forward and dug into one of the many pouches on my leather belt. I pulled out a small plastic sphere and without turning around, threw it over my shoulder, crushing it as I did so.

The smell only just reached me as I propelled myself away from the stink bomb. I heard coughing and spluttering behind me, and as I reached the doors to the stair-well, I risked a glance over my shoulder. There were three of them now, two guys and a girl, and throwing a bad smell at them had not slowed them down.

I took the stairs two at a time, trying to take deep breaths, the book heavy in my grip.

It's gonna be worth it, Lily. Totally worth it, I thought.

The wide, spiraling staircase opened out onto a new hallway at the top, and right at the end of the corridor were the large exit doors.

I dipped my hand into a different pouch and pulled out a handful of ball bearings. Once I had put a few feet between myself and the staircase, I dumped them on the carpeted floor behind me. A second later, I heard a yelp, and then a thud. This time, I didn't risk a look back. I pictured my sister's sleeping face and ran as fast as my malnourished ass would carry me.

I reached the doors, twisting my body and throwing my shoulder against them to keep as much momentum as I could. I blinked as I stumbled into the bright light, momentarily disoriented before the vista of the Oxford street on a sunny day settled before me.

"Stop her!" The librarian's voice was loud enough through the open doors that a few people passing by paused and looked at me. I pivoted, trying to find the direction of the road I'd parked my shit-heap car on.

A tall woman in yoga pants and a vest turned to me, frowning. Her eyes moved to the leatherbound book under my arm, and she took a step closer. From my peripheral vision, I caught the motion of a figure bursting out of the museum doors.

I drew on what little strength I had left and sprinted down the road to my right.

Please be the right road, please be the right road, I chanted in my head, too out of breath to make the plea aloud.

A vision of my sister wearing her scolding face filled my head. *You should remember these things, Almi! You're always making life difficult for yourself!* The mental image of Lily spoke firmly, and I sucked as much strength from her as I could as I pelted down the leafy street.

All the roads in the university area of Oxford looked the same to me, and I had no idea if I was racing along the one I'd actually parked my car in. Praying I was, I dug into another pouch on my belt and yanked my car keys out. I could hear footsteps pounding behind me.

Might be time to use the big guns, said Lily in my head. *Get the elephant projector.*

I bared my teeth through my panting breaths. Reluctantly, I pulled the most expensive weapon I had from my belt. It was a small plastic box, not much bigger than a credit card, and it had taken me days to work out how to use it in my cramped little trailer. Not to mention the effort to steal the thing in the first place.

My attention snagged on something thirty feet in front of me. A small, rusty yellow Ford. *My car.*

There was no way I could unlock it, get in it, and start it, without the hunky librarians catching up to me, I conceded. I would have to use the elephant projector.

Pressing the little button on it, I launched it over my shoulder. I heard the clatter of plastic on asphalt, then a small cry. The footsteps stopped, and I launched myself at my car door. I rammed the key in the lock, cursing the fact that my ancient car didn't have remote locking. It didn't even have a certificate to say it was roadworthy. As the handle clicked open and I threw myself into the driver's seat, I saw two librarians staring, bewildered, at a massive hologram of an elephant, throwing its trunk in the air and rearing up onto its back legs.

It would only distract them for a few seconds. If I could have fitted decent speakers in the little device, I could have made it better. But I didn't have the money for speakers. Hell, I didn't have the money for anything.

I turned the key in the ignition, squeezing my eyes closed and pleading for the rust-bucket to start. I gave an involuntary squeal of relief as the engine roared to life, and the two librarians stopped squinting at the electronic elephant to snap their eyes to mine through the windshield. I gulped, rammed the car into gear, and put my foot on the gas.

"Shit. That was close," I said aloud as I pulled onto the freeway. Adrenaline was buzzing through me, and my lungs still burned. I was used to being hungry, but I wasn't used to being hungry *and* doing a bad impression of an athlete.

Too close. You really should have remembered where you parked the car, Lily said. I always saw her in my mind with vivid blue hair and shimmering skin. The way she had looked *before*.

Before she fell unconscious. Before I was sent away and hidden in the human world.

My exile hadn't stopped me trying to wake my sister up though. And after years of research, I finally knew where I might find the answers to curing her sickness.

This book was the key. This book was going to tell me what I needed to save her.

CHAPTER 2

It was almost dark by the time I pulled into the trailer park I reluctantly called home. In England, they called it a caravan park, but when I'd first been dumped in the mortal world, I had found myself in California, USA, and that's where I'd tried to learn how to fit into a world without magic.

I had been born in Olympus, a world where the Greek gods ruled, and magic and mythology was as real, and as dangerous, as it could be.

Home was the underwater realm of Aquarius, and the first thing I had done when I found myself stranded in America, was try to find a way back there. A way back to my sister, so that I could cure her sleeping sickness.

Back then, in my lowest moments, I'd wondered if I'd invented my home world, just to escape the shitty reality of my life.

That was when Lily had begun talking to me in my head. At first, I had assumed I was going crazy from grief and frustration. But I'd started to wonder if it really was her, talking to me through some mystical sibling bond.

After all, before she fell unconscious, Lily had been one of the most powerful sea nymphs I knew.

This is it, Lily. This time, I'm sure, I told her as I switched off the ignition.

I grabbed the book and my backpack, climbed out of the car and let myself into my trailer. I called her Betty Blue, because she had a blue stripe around the top of her peeling fiber-glass hull. There were six bolts on Betty Blue's unassuming door to unlock - all discreetly installed so it didn't look like there was anything inside worth stealing to my less-than-savory neighbors.

Truth was, there was plenty worth stealing - most of it stolen by me in the first place.

I had a decent moral compass, but my need to get home and save my sister was greater than my distaste for breaking the rules. I had only stolen things I really needed, and nothing of sentimental value to anyone, or that couldn't be replaced. And only stuff I could never afford, no matter how many hours I put in at cafes, bars, supermarkets - and anywhere else a girl could get casual work with no bank account. I bought food and paid the rental on Betty Blue with honest cash, but the rest…

It had taken me a few years to find my first Olympus artifact in the human realm, which I had subsequently stolen.

I looked over at the metafora compass hanging on a peg on the wall after I locked the trailer door behind me and flipped on the lights. It allowed me to move between the human realm and Olympus, and it was worth a fortune. Not that I would ever part with it.

It only had three uses, and I was down to just one left.

Moving to the bed at the back of the trailer, I pulled my sketchbook out from under my pillow. It wasn't actually my sketchbook, it was Lily's. But other than the compass, it was the most valuable thing I owned.

Drawing in the little book transferred a memory to it, to be relived as and when one liked, and Lily had used it when I was a child so she could show me her memories of our mother. Through it, I had been able to see exactly what our mom had been like, at least through Lily's eyes.

I had taken the book with me when I'd been exiled from Olympus as a way to be closer to her, but I'd found myself so overwhelmed by my own thoughts that I'd begun drawing my memories into the book too.

My sketches were crap compared to hers, but it seemed to work all the same.

I flipped the pages until I saw a rough pencil sketch of a woman lying in a bed. Blotches that had once been tears smeared the drawing, but it didn't stop it from working. Swallowing, I touched the sketch.

It heated under my fingertips, and I was no longer in the trailer. Instead, I was standing in a small bedroom in a house that wasn't mine.

This was an image I knew wasn't projected by some

grief-stricken part of my psyche. This image was real; my own memory of the last time I had seen my sister.

There, lying on a narrow bed, was Lily. I watched her a moment. No breath came from her lips, and there was no shine on her sallow skin. Her blue hair was dull, and her eyes were closed. I knew that if I could reach out and touch her, she would be as cold as ice. For all intents and purposes, she could be dead.

But she was alive. The Oracle had said as much before I'd been dragged away.

'The Nereid will sleep, until the gods weep.'

Tears of frustration burned at the back of my eyes as I stared uselessly at Lily's image. "Fucking Oracle," I spat, and the image faded, the trailer returning around me.

It's not her fault, my mental projection of Lily said gently.

"It's someone's fault."

Maybe.

One tear leaked down my cheek and I scrubbed it away angrily. Before I could stop myself, I was flipping back the pages of the sketchbook.

You don't need to see it again, said Lily.

"There might be something I missed before." There was an edge of desperation to my voice.

Almi... Lily's voice faded away as I touched a sketch of a platform floating on the sea, a line of indistinct, badly drawn stick figures standing on it. My fingers felt hot, and then I was eighteen again.

CHAPTER 3

*E*IGHT YEARS AGO, IN POSEIDON'S REALM OF AQUARIUS

"Tell me again why we're here?" I hissed to my sister under my breath.

"Shhhh." Lily stared ahead, avoiding my look.

I scowled. Lily had spent her whole life telling me to stay under the radar, make sure nobody knew that I was… broken. Powerless. Able to do *nothing* with magic. I couldn't even sense it.

"It could be the death of you if anyone finds out," she had told me. *"We must do whatever it takes to keep it a secret. Nobody must know."*

And yet, there we were on my eighteenth birthday, lined up with two-hundred other sea nymphs on a giant floating dais in the middle the sea, being inspected by the king of the ocean himself. The almighty, and utterly terrifying, Poseidon.

I leaned forward just an inch, looking past the other women in the line, to peer at the god.

He was seven feet tall, at least, with long white hair loose over enormous shoulders. I couldn't see his face, but I could see that he was wearing a robe that looked like the ocean, aqua and turquoise waves crashing over the fabric as he solemnly made his way down the line of women.

"This is bullshit," I whispered to Lily.

"Almi! Be quiet!" She finally broke her stare ahead and glared at me. "This is serious. Poseidon called us here, and we have to answer. Now, behave."

She loaded the command with so much uncharacteristic authority, I shut my mouth.

Lily had been playing the role of my mom for as long as I could remember, but she wasn't very strict. Mostly, she left me alone to mess around with things that covered up the fact that I had no magic, while she honed her own considerable power at the Academy. Lily was everything I wasn't. She was beautiful, with bright blue hair, skin that shone like mother-of-pearl, and a tattoo of a nautilus shell across her chest that was so vividly colored I never tired of looking at it. And she had an almost godly magic over water. She was a true representative of our kind. Of the Nereid.

I, on the other hand, had dark hair with the tiniest hint of blue, pale skin from being inside so much, and my shell tattoo was just a thin black outline. No color at all. No color, and no magic.

I sighed and peered out to get another glimpse of Poseidon.

My breath caught as I turned my head and looked straight into the bluest eyes I had ever seen.

Not just blue… They were every hue of the ocean, and silver swirled amongst the greens and blues, drawing me in, taking me deeper-

"Your name?" The ocean god barked.

Power washed over me as Poseidon approached, but unlike Lily's power, which felt like a light breeze across the ocean, carrying the faint tang of salt, his power was heavy, oppressive even. Whirlpools swirled in my mind, dark crashing waves dragging down everything in their path as they tore through my head.

Oh gods. Oh gods.

I'd forgotten my own name.

Poseidon took a step toward me, holding my panicked gaze, and I felt Lily stiffen beside me.

"Lily," I gasped, pulling on the only name I could remember.

"You would lie to your king?" His voice was an echo of thunder over a stormy ocean, and I couldn't breathe properly.

He stopped before me, the fabric of his robe flowing, muscular shoulders widening. Entrancing blue eyes churning with volatile power.

"I-" I choked. But his magic was overwhelming. The skies seemed to darken behind him.

"She is young," Lily said, her calm voice cutting through the storm. I saw her bow her head in my peripheral vision as I tried to suck in air. "My apologies, my king."

Poseidon finally removed his gaze from me, and the air flowed easier into my chest.

"What kind of nymph are you?" he asked my sister.

She hesitated a second before answering. "Nereid."

This time, Poseidon stiffened. He held his hand up, his fingers fluttering as though feeling for her power in the air. "You speak the truth," he murmured. His eyes moved back to mine, but this time my throat didn't close.

When he continued to stare at me, I nodded. His eyes were mesmerizing, and I was struggling to concentrate on anything else.

"You are aware of the prophecy from Apollo's Oracle at Delphi?" His voice was a hoarse whisper.

I looked to Lily, confused, and she shook her head. "No, my king."

He flicked his wrist, and a white flame burst from his hand. When it died away, there was an image left behind. A woman with dark skin, wrapped in layers and layers of cloth, and only her youthful face showing, was chanting nonsensical words. Her eyelids fluttered open to reveal pure white eyes. I instinctively reached for my sister's hand, and I felt her grip mine back.

"He who possesses the heart of a Nereid shall possess the Heart of the Ocean. True love is not a necessity, pure possession will seal the deal." The woman's eyes rolled in her head, and tendrils of red began to bleed and spread across the milky white.

I squeezed Lily's hand harder.

"But be warned. True love will never go unnoticed. Should-"

ELIZA RAINE & ROSE WILSON

Poseidon flicked his hand again, and the image vanished before the woman finished the sentence.

Lily drew in a deep breath, and I felt her hand shaking around mine.

"You have never heard this prophecy before?" Poseidon asked.

"No, my king."

"You are what I have been seeking." His tone had turned steely, and Lily gripped my hand so hard it hurt. Fear spread through me as I looked at her frightened face. Lily was never frightened.

"How do you possess someone's heart?" I couldn't help the question from tumbling from my lips, though my voice was barely a whisper. Surely Poseidon, one of the three most powerful gods in the whole of Olympus, wasn't about to cut out our hearts?

The god locked his eyes on mine again. "Marriage," he said, eventually.

I thought that would have lessened my sister's fear - relief that our hearts were staying firmly within our chests was coursing through me. But her hand continued to shake.

"That was the purpose of today?" Lily asked. "To find a Nereid?"

"There are very, very few of you left. In fact, you two might be the last."

Sadness jolted through me at his words. Lily had always been evasive when I asked about our kind, but I didn't think she had known we were the last.

"And now?"

"You will address me as your king." His words were

14

firm, but the lethal power lacing his voice when he had first approached us was gone.

He lifted his hand again, and all the other women gawking at us on the floating marble platform vanished. "I will return tomorrow. And I will wed one of you. I care not which."

There was a flash of light, and we were back in our home.

"What just happened?" I stared at my sister, my mind reeling as she stumbled backward and collapsed into one of the squishy armchairs in our small living area. Her eyes were wide with fright, and I moved to her, bending to throw my arms around her. She was stiff for a moment, then she wrapped her arms around me, pulling me tight against her.

"Oh, Almi. I'm sorry. We shouldn't have gone."

"Did you know about that prophecy?" I pulled back, looking into her eyes. They were misty with unshed tears as she shook her head.

"I knew that the women of our kind were hunted over the years, but I never knew why. I knew that nobody could know that you were vulnerable, and that we had to be strong to defend ourselves. I didn't know that *possession of our hearts* was the reason." She looked sick as she spoke the word possession. "But... But there is no defense from Poseidon. He is a king and a god."

And not just any god.

Olympus was divided into twelve realms, each ruled

over by an Olympian god, and the three strongest were the brothers who ruled the Underworld, the Sky, and the Sea.

Hades, Zeus, and Poseidon.

"Did he really say marriage?" I breathed.

Lily nodded. "Yes."

I frowned, trying to work that through. "Would that make whoever married him a queen?"

"Yes. A queen in a gilded cage."

"Queens have power and wealth. We would be protected." I was trying to see a bright side, but when I remembered how the god had made me feel, the dark, stormy, drowning waves of power he'd sent through me, I shuddered.

"Almi, we should marry for love, not be forced into it! What of sharing a bed? Would you give that away to someone you didn't love, for a lifetime?"

"No," I said, shaking my head. I had yet to experience any kind of physical love, but I knew I wanted to be the one to choose.

"We would be beholden. Trapped. Creatures of the ocean are not meant to be trapped." She drew in a long breath and stood up out of her chair. She began to pace the small room we'd lived in most of my life.

"I'm not a creature of the ocean," I said, aware of how small my voice was. I tried to make it stronger. "I'll do it."

Tears spilled from Lily's eyes as she turned back to me. "Of course you won't."

"I will. It makes no difference to me. I have no future in Aquarius anyway. Not without any magic. I don't feel the call of the ocean like you, or have the potential to change the world." I forced a smile onto my face. "I'll do it."

"Almi, it's exactly *because* you have no power that I can't let you do that. If he found out, I don't know what he would do."

I swallowed, knowing I couldn't keep the question clawing its way out of my throat in. It was the same question I asked my sister whenever I couldn't understand why I was broken. "Am… Am I really a Nereid?"

Lily gathered me up in her arms again. "We've been through this. Of course you are. You think I put that shell tattoo on your chest, silly?"

"You could have," I mumbled into her shoulder.

"Well, I didn't. I don't know why you don't have your colors or your magic. But they will come one day. And you will not be the trophy wife of an arrogant, entitled god, I swear." She kissed me on the top of the head, her blue hair falling over my brown.

"I love you, Lily."

"I know. I love you too."

"What are we going to do?"

"We can't run. Not from one of the three most powerful beings in the world."

"So...?"

She sighed against my head, all the breath leaving her body. "So, I marry in the morning."

I squeezed her. "I mean it, Lily. I'll do it. You could do so much good with your magic."

"No, Almi. He can never know that you don't have your power. That's our secret, okay? And you never know, maybe I can do more good from the palace. And maybe

Poseidon will not turn out to have a heart of ice." Her voice turned bitter, and I pushed back to look into her face.

"Is that where we'll live? In the palace?"

She nodded. "I assume so."

"I'll come with you, won't I?"

Her soft features hardened. "That will be my only stipulation."

"What if he says no?" Tears filled my eyes at the thought of being separated from Lily.

She brushed my cheek and smiled. "Nothing will keep us apart, I promise."

CHAPTER 4

*T*he trailer appeared around me, the memory fading before I could feel the pain of reliving what happened next.

Anything new? Lily asked.

"No. Poseidon is still an asshole."

You say that every time. I don't know why you do it to yourself.

"I can't help it," I muttered. Maybe I was a masochist. Maybe I needed the constant burn of anger to keep me going. After all, he was the one who had exiled me, and was the reason I had to hide in the mortal world.

"Book," I said firmly, shaking my head and dragging my hand over my face.

I pulled the book I'd so nearly been caught stealing from the bench onto my lap.

My heart beat fast, and butterflies fluttered in my stomach as I ran my fingertips over it. *Please. Please be the final piece.*

After I'd found the metafora compass, I spent the

following five years hunting for anything that could help Lily. It was amazing how many Olympus artifacts had been hidden in the human world—just like me. Eventually, I'd followed the breadcrumbs of magical items to Oxford, England, and this book.

When I flipped open the leather cover, I saw the drawing that I'd hoped would be there. A map of Olympus.

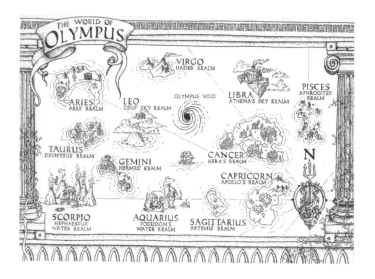

I recognized it from my own childhood. I hadn't been able to attend the Academy to learn to use my power or be educated in the ways of Olympus, but Lily had, and she'd shared a lot of what she'd learned with me, including this map.

Guilt twanged through me as I remembered what a brat I had been to my sister sometimes, bitter about my lack of magic - and jealous of hers. If Lily had ever resented having to take on the role of my mother and deal with my shit, she had never shown it.

I had always been too busy tinkering with artifacts and chemicals and things that I thought would cover up my being broken, to really appreciate what she did for me.

I refocused on the map before me, my finger moving of its own volition to touch the little representation of Aquarius. There was one other water realm - Hephaestus' underwater volcano world, Scorpio. There were two realms that floated in the sky, Athena's Libra, and Zeus' Leo, and the rest of the gods' realms were islands.

I scanned the map one more time to make sure I couldn't see what I was looking for.

A secret realm.

A realm that didn't appear on any map, but that the scriptures I had found in Germany suggested was the birthplace of my kind. And not just the Nereid. If the scriptures were to be believed, and I had no reason to doubt their authenticity, then the fabled realm was the birthplace of many of the creatures that lived in Olympus, and more importantly - the location of incredible healing magic.

The scriptures stated that the realm was hidden by the gods so it couldn't be abused by those with power. I didn't know what that meant, yet, but they had also said that the only way to find the realm was with a book devoted to navigating the world of the gods.

The book had I just stolen from a museum in Oxford.

"Please, please tell me how to cure my sister," I pleaded aloud, before turning the page and whistling a sigh of relief to see that the hand-scrawled text was in a language I could read.

"Knowledge is power, blah, blah, blah," I mumbled as I skimmed through the writing, eager to get to something useful.

"Ah!" I jammed my finger down on the fourth page, pulse quickening. "The Font of Zoi in the realm of Atlantis was the source of a great deal of life in Olympus and retains the power to heal all manner of ailments."

I kept reading. "If the font is used for ill purpose, then grave consequences shall befall those involved." I nodded. I had come across a writing two years ago that suggested that healing artifacts could backfire as often as they helped, often due to the intention of the user. Dark intentions equaled dark magic.

"A magic like this must be controlled, as with enough strength and commitment, new life could potentially be created, perhaps with disastrous consequences. The Font of Zoi should only ever be used to create life if a species is in mortal danger."

A little giddy with hope, I read on.

"This is a dangerous and involved magic, only possible in certain circumstances. See more in the book of mageía." I hissed out my disappointment. That was a book I had never heard of.

I flicked through the pages, looking for anything about Atlantis. There was a large group of pages about the four forbidden realms of Olympus, and then a long chapter about the colossal mountain that Zeus' sky realm ringed. After that I found an interesting but unhelpful few chapters on weather and seasonality in the various realms.

Next was the section on the two ocean realms. I found myself slowing down when I read the part about Aquarius, mumbling the words as I read.

"Aquarius is made up of undersea domes that most often glow faintly with gold. The bulk of the realm is made up of around two hundred of these domes connected by clear tunnels, but there are many parts of Aquarius that lie separate from the main body. Poseidon's Palace, for example, is in its own dome, and can only be reached by crossing clear ocean."

I scowled at the mention of the ocean god.

"Some domes have towers that rise up so high they penetrate the surface of the ocean, with stables at the top to house pegasi. Created by Poseidon, these winged horses prefer to live close to the waves, but need to be able to fly, so the stable towers allow them this."

There had been a pegasus tower near where Lily and I had lived, and Lily told me that they offered flying lessons at the academy once. She hadn't been interested in flying, but I couldn't recall ever being more jealous of her.

"There are also many creatures confined to the depths of the ocean, far beneath the dome cities. These creatures are giant, deadly, and some say, so horrific to lay eyes upon that they could send a weak mind mad. Poseidon is the only god who can keep them at bay. It is believed by this author that the ocean god has put these creatures to work to guard the realm of Atlantis."

For a second, I was sure my heart had stopped beating altogether.

I read the line again.

Poseidon's creatures of the depths were guarding the lost realm?

Excitement warred with fear. How in the name of all the gods was I going to get past Poseidon's sea monsters?

The irony was that Lily, with her fiercely strong water magic, might actually have had a chance. But me? I was barely even a decent swimmer, for god's sake. Where Lily could hold her breath for almost half an hour underwater, as a sea nymph *should* be able to, I struggled after five minutes. Anger and frustration welled up inside me, and I took a deep breath.

Focusing on the page, I read on.

"The reason for this belief is that Poseidon was witnessed on two occasions taking lesser beings far, far below his realm, to depths that should not be possible to survive, yet they returned safe and healthy. Poseidon undertook these ventures on his ship, the *okeánios ánemos*. Pulled by horses made of enchanted water, his is the only ship in Olympus that can move through water, and so, no one other than the god of the ocean himself can reach the pitch-dark depths below Aquarius. This makes for the perfect hiding place for the realm of Atlantis."

My eyes darted further down the page, but the author moved on to the subject of the rest of the ships in Olympus, which unlike human ships did not sail on the surface of water but flew through the sky to move between realms.

I went back and reread the relevant passage until my eyes blurred, my pulse racing.

"Lily, it looks like I'm going to have to up my game," I breathed eventually. "I've got a ship to steal."

I took a deep breath as I looked around my little trailer an hour later.

With any luck, this would be the last time I would see its drafty interior. It had been my home, though, and a small part of me would be sad not to see it again. A much larger part of me couldn't wait to get back to Olympus.

I had everything packed in my bag, and I was holding the metafora compass in my hand.

The little bronze object looked just like a normal compass, except instead of North, East, West, and South on the face, the needle could move between various Greek words. I didn't know the meaning of them all, but I knew the most important one.

Spíti. *Home.*

I had last been home six years ago, when I first found the compass. I hadn't been able to resist seeing Lily. I had only spent a few days there, and I'd been terrified of being caught by the merciless Poseidon the whole time.

I told nobody about my return, not even my best friend, who was keeping Lily's unconscious form safe in his home. Sneaking past him to see her had felt like a betrayal, but I hadn't known what Poseidon would do if he had caught me, and I didn't want to risk my friend's safety.

I'd used the compass to return to the human world, hellbent on finding a way to cure Lily before I used it to return to her.

And now I had one.

I was one-hundred-percent sure that I trusted the information that I had gleaned from the book. And if I was being honest, I had no other leads.

This was the final trip I would make with the compass.

And this time, I couldn't be scared of Poseidon.

I was going to steal his damned ship, sail it to the depths below Aquarius, and find Atlantis and its healing magic. I hadn't worked out how I would get past the sea monsters or use the healing magic yet - but first thing was first, I had to find the ship. And that meant getting into Poseidon's Palace.

That would be a feat for most people. But for me? Damn near impossible. The Palace was the home of the god who had banished me from Olympus, and the only person who knew who I really was. Poseidon's Palace was literally the last place in Olympus I should be going, but that was exactly what I was going to do.

Just as soon as I'd seen Lily.

"Thanks for everything, Betty Blue," I said, touching the Formica countertop fondly. I clutched the bronze compass, my stomach flipping over with excited trepidation. "Spíti," I said on a breath. *Take me home.*

I barely had time to finish the thought before the whole world disappeared around me.

CHAPTER 5

I felt the bronze compass fall from my hand, then heard it clatter as the freezing wind that had just whipped around me vanished. My hair was a mess in front of my face, and I was vaguely aware I'd dropped to one knee. Chatter and loud voices filtered through to me as the spinning sensation lessened enough that I could stand and push my hair out of my eyes.

I wasn't in Betty Blue anymore.

In fact, I wasn't in the mortal realm anymore.

Slowly I tipped my head back, looking up. Praying, praying, praying that I wouldn't see sky above me, but that I would see-

"Water," I gasped.

Aquarius.

Far above my head was a faintly shimmering veil of gold, and beyond that, miles of blue ocean. The silhouette of a pod of whales was visible against the bright light of the surface, and closer to the gold shield overhead I could see dolphins playing as they sped along through the water.

I was in a gleaming, golden underwater dome of Aquarius.

I lowered my gaze, forcing myself to breathe deeply but my head dizzy with relief and excitement.

Buildings made from rusty-colored sand mixed with larger, shining white stone structures all the way up to the gleaming gold dome edge in the distance. Just in front of me was a large clearing filled with a bustling marketplace. People moved between the canvas stalls, and I stared. They weren't all human. Some had wings. Others had tails. Some were blue-skinned.

I turned slowly, looking for anything that would confirm that this was the market-town I had grown up in. The temperature was perfect, and despite being underwater there was a slight, salty breeze that I sucked in gratefully as I scanned my surroundings.

'Fyki Tanners' read a small wooden board outside a building with rails of leather hanging outside. Tears burned at the back of my eyes.

"I'm home," I breathed.

For good, this time.

"You dropped this, dearie," said a husky female voice, and I spun to see an older woman in a beautiful gold robe holding out the compass to me.

I blinked at her a few times, and she frowned. "Are you alright?"

"Yes," I answered, reaching for the compass. "Yes, thank you. Is this... Am I in Fyki?"

I knew I was. But I wanted to hear someone say it.

"Yes, dearie. Do you need somewhere to stay? There's a lovely taverna here, or a cheaper one in the next dome along." Her eyes scanned my crappy clothes as she mentioned the cheaper taverna, but I barely heard her.

"Is the bakery still here?"

She raised her eyebrow. "There are two bakeries in Fyki."

"Silos' bakery."

"Over there, beyond that row of stalls."

"Thank you," I breathed, and then my legs were moving. I'd broken into a run before I knew it.

I burst through the door of the bakery, heart pounding and mind racing.

I was back. I was in frigging Olympus.

"We're closed!" shouted a deep male voice. "Come back tomorrow." I moved to the counter, hardly seeing the empty shelves where the bread should be.

"Silos?" I called, directing my voice at the door that led to the kilns.

I heard banging and then a curse.

"I said we're closed," the man snapped.

"It's Almi."

There was another loud bang, then footsteps. A second later, a tall, dark man in a leather apron and scruffy hair appeared in the doorway.

His mouth fell open, then slowly formed a disbelieving smile. "Almi! Where in the name of the gods have you been?"

29

An almighty wave of emotion crashed over me as I smiled back at the boy who had been my best friend for my whole childhood.

"You have her safe, right?"

"Of course." He rushed forward, wiping his hands on his apron, and lifted a hinged part of the counter. As he pulled me into a hug, the burn of tears behind my eyes returned.

He may not look like the boy I had left behind anymore, but he smelled like the world I had been taken from. Familiar and safe.

"Take me to her," I said, pulling back from him.

"I can't believe you're back," he breathed, then nodded, his too-long hair falling over his forehead. "Come on."

Silos lead me through the back of the bakery and up a narrow flight of stairs. I held my breath as we passed two doors at the top, and he pushed open a third.

I didn't even try to stop the tears from spilling out when I saw Lily in the little bed.

I was at her side in a heartbeat, overwhelming emotions pulling me in different directions. Joy to be beside her. Devastation to see her as lifeless as my memory in the sketchbook.

Her skin was as ice-cold as I knew it would be when I ran my fingers down her face.

"Lily. Oh Lily, I'm going to fix this." I pressed my forehead to hers, my tears spilling onto her cheeks. "I'm back now. I got back to you. We're together again."

I wasn't sure how long I stayed with her, but eventually I heard Silos cough gently. I turned to him.

"I can't tell you how grateful I am to you, Silos. For taking care of her all these years."

He shrugged awkwardly. "I mean, she doesn't need much." His expression changed and he shook his hands vigorously, like he'd said something offensive. "Ah shit, I didn't mean, you know, just, she's..." He trailed off, wincing.

"It's okay. I know."

"There's, erm, something you might not know." His voice was grave, and he looked even more awkward as he stepped through the doorway and into the room. I was sitting on the floor by the raised pallet that functioned as Lily's bed, and he crouched down beside me.

He reached out and moved the blankets back. She was fully clothed under the sheets, and we both knew the blankets made no difference to her wellbeing, but it felt right to have them there.

"I'm sorry, Almi. But I noticed this a few months ago."

I tracked my eyes over her, looking for something wrong. "Her hands..."

I stared, my stomach dropping. Lily's skin used to shine like mother-of-pearl. But now... Now her skin was turning to stone.

Through fresh tears, I forced myself to look at her fingers, to touch them.

Cold, hard, stone.

"What's happening to her?"

"I don't know. Her feet are the same. I..." Silos swallowed. "I haven't checked anywhere else, I wasn't sure-"

I cut him off, laying a hand on his shoulder as hot tears

tracked down my face. He looked at me, dark eyes filled with sympathy.

"I didn't know if you'd ever come back, but if you did, this wasn't what I wanted you to come back to," he said quietly.

"I'm going to fix this," I said, forcing myself to my feet.

Silos stood with me. "Do you know how?"

I shook my head. "No. But I know where to start."

"Okay. First things first," Silos said as he placed two tankards down on the kitchen table, then sat down opposite me.

I took a swig of the drink, wincing with both shock and delight at the taste.

"Man, I'd forgotten how good this is," I said.

"Never mind the mead, tell me where you've been! All I know is that you show up with the fucking King of the Ocean one day, tell me your sister is in a magical sleep, ask me to take care of her, and then vanish!"

I gave him a look. "You were there. You know I didn't choose to vanish."

He took a swig of his own drink. "I have replayed the conversation you had with Poseidon over in my head so many times."

"You and me both," I growled. I'd watched it a hundred times since.

"Why did Poseidon send you away? Where did he send you? How did Lily end up like...*that*?"

I blew out a breath. "I can't tell you why he sent me away. As for where? The human world."

Silos' eyes widened. "No magic?"

I shook my head. "No magic." Silos didn't know I had no magic myself. Nobody except Lily knew that.

"Well, that explains whatever it is that you're wearing." He scowled at my outfit and I looked down. I guessed jeans and a Rolling Stones t-shirt weren't going to help me fit in in Aquarius.

"Do you have clothes I can borrow?"

"I can find something, sure," he said. "And Lily? How did she get like that?"

"I don't know." I glared at my drink, then downed a big gulp.

Silos took another deep swig of his drink too. "Almi, honestly, I'm so pleased to see you."

The truth of his words showed in his eyes, and I swallowed down my emotion. If I let it bubble up, it would overwhelm me. I was teetering on a precipice - utter joy that I was back in Olympus versus fierce focus and determination to save Lily.

I couldn't go to pieces. Not yet. Especially now she appeared to be turning to stone. I squashed my nausea at the thought and sipped more mead before answering him.

"I'm glad to be back. And I meant what I said, about you keeping her safe. It's kept me going, all these years. Thank you."

"That's what friends do." His eyes roamed over me, as though he still wasn't fully sure I was real. "You look different."

I laughed. "So do you."

33

His dark skin deepened in color. "Yeah. I got a bit taller."

"Just a bit."

"But you… Your hair isn't blue anymore."

"No. It turned fully dark when I entered the human world." Maybe it would turn back, now I was in Olympus again, but it had never been as vibrant as my sister's.

"Do you have somewhere to stay?"

I shook my head. "Could I stay here with Lily? Just until I get sorted."

"Sure."

I hesitated a moment, then asked a question of my own. "Where's your dad?"

Silos' eyes lit up. "He got a job in the palace."

"Huh. That's great." *Great if you wanted to be anywhere near the fuckwit that was Poseidon,* I added in my head.

"Yeah, he loves it. Best bread in Aquarius, fit for royalty," Silos beamed proudly.

I gave him a genuine smile back. "Your family always made the best bread."

"Yup. It was hard running this place on my own at first, but I'm good now."

"I'm sure you're doing great." And I meant it. Silos was as resourceful as I was. In fact, we'd met raiding the same trash for tossed out bits of junk that we could turn into something amazing.

"Thanks. Was it Poseidon who brought you back?"

"Hell no."

"Then how did you get here?"

"A metafora compass."

Silos stared at me. "How did you afford one of those?"

"I, erm , didn't."

Silos laughed. "Say no more."

I drained the rest of my mead, trying to work out how much to tell him. My brain was foggy, though, and I was starting to feel the first whack of fatigue hit me. The adrenaline buzzing through my body was wearing off, and it was getting harder to fight my emotions.

"Do you mind if I go upstairs?"

"Of course not. I'll get you some blankets and a pillow. Is there anything else you want?"

I gave him a grin. "You got any bread?"

CHAPTER 6

"*A*lmi, you can't be serious. You want to steal from Poseidon?" Silos was working at the counter, kneading dough and throwing me disbelieving glances over his shoulder as he worked the next morning.

I'd slept, badly, on the floor of Lily's room, unable to keep checking her limbs, her stone fingers and toes making me feel unwell. *I had almost been too late.* I couldn't shift the awful thought that if I'd taken just a few months longer to come home, she could have been a freaking statue of herself.

Most of my wakeful moments had been spent wrangling my guilt into determination.

I was home now, and I was going to save her. Going to pieces, crying, or wallowing in remorse would do nothing for her. Stealing Poseidon's ship and finding the Font of Zoi would help her.

"I'm deadly serious," I answered Silos. "It's the only way to cure Lily."

I'd realized overnight that I would have to let Silos

into at least a little of my plan, as he knew far more about Aquarius and the palace than I did. I would be hindering myself by not asking for his help.

"Are you going to tell me what it is you want to steal?"

"No." I shook my head. "The less you know, the better. If your dad works at the Palace, then you must be able to get in to visit him?"

"No, I haven't ever been to see him at the Palace. Dad comes and visits here every three months. Almi, Poseidon sent you away - you shouldn't risk him finding out you're back, let alone getting caught stealing from him. He's merciless with criminals."

I shrugged, the movement far more casual than I felt. Poseidon was merciless, period. I knew that firsthand. "The Palace is huge. I'm sure Poseidon would never even know I was there."

Except, I had history with the god, and I was pretty sure he'd recognize me instantly, blue hair or not.

I would have to risk it, though. I needed to find out where he kept his ship. I knew I wouldn't be able to just walk in and take it - plans would have to be made.

"How can I get a job at the Palace?" I asked.

Silos looked over his shoulder at me, eyebrows raised. "You can't. I mean, short of entering the competition to be his personal guard." He snorted as he slapped more dough down on the countertop and began to beat it.

"What?"

"Nothing. It was a joke."

"Tell me."

"Every twenty years, he runs the Poseidon Trials, to

recruit members for his personal guard. The competition starts in a few days."

"A few days?"

Slowly, Silos turned to face me. "Almi, people die in the Poseidon Trials. We're too young to remember the last one, but my friend told me the other day that all but two of the entrants were killed."

When I didn't reply, he shook his head and wiped his brow, smearing flour across his face.

"Only the elite enter. The strongest of the strong, the most magic of the magic. *Heroes.*"

I still just stared at him, my mind whirring. I didn't have magic. I was undernourished and out of shape. *Elite* was not a word I would use to describe myself. But I was smart. And I had a few days to arm myself with gadgets and artifacts to help me.

Besides, I didn't have to win. All I had to do was stay alive long enough to find a way to steal the ship. If nothing else, I was a tenacious sonofabitch - I could survive a few days, surely? If I was lucky, his magical ship was actually in the palace somewhere.

"Almi... They wouldn't even let you enter the competition. You have to have a reason. A connection to Poseidon, or crazy strong water magic, or be sponsored by another god."

"I do have a connection to Poseidon," I said quietly.

"Yeah, and I wish you'd tell me what it is," Silos said, his expression dark and serious now.

"How do I sign up?"

"You can't." Silos folded his arms across his chest.

I folded mine to match. "Watch me."

I left the bakery, rucksack over my shoulder and wearing an Aquarius-appropriate linen shirt. I couldn't help the ripples of excitement I felt as I reached the marketplace, the big blue ocean overhead and the dome edges gleaming gold in the distance.

I had spent the last eight years around human technology, which nobody could deny had a hell of a lot going for it, but here in Aquarius... The wares being sold at the stalls I was walking past were *magic*. And magic was just what I needed.

There was no question that swimming and water magic would be required to survive the Poseidon Trials. The truth was that even *getting* to Poseidon's palace was a pain in the ass for me. I could swim, but only as well as your average human. Which was *not* good enough to cross the expanse of freezing open water between the main city of domes and the one housing the underwater castle in which the asshole god lived.

Fortunately, Aquarius did have human - and non-swimming - inhabitants, so there were a variety of ways to help them maneuver between the domes that were not connected by tunnels. The problem was, I had to convince everyone that I was super-powerful, and that would be hard if I couldn't cross half a mile of water by myself.

If I wanted to make the right impression and hide my utter lack of magic, I would have to find a way to get to the palace in style. And that meant finding a way to breathe underwater and swim much better than I currently could.

. . .

I stopped at a stall on my right, scanning the bright powders and jars of fizzing liquids.

"All sorts of healing here, dearie," the man behind the stall said to me. I looked up at him and realized he wasn't a man at all, but some sort of griffin hybrid, with a beak for a nose and leathery looking wings behind him. I couldn't see his legs but knew they would look like they belonged on a lion.

"You got anything... destructive?" I asked hopefully.

He grinned at me, eyes crinkling above his beak. "Oh yes. What did you have in mind?"

It took me an hour to load up on all the supplies I needed. I had been relieved to find that some of my human gadgets were rare enough in Olympus that I was able to trade them for some of the more expensive magical items. A broken cellphone for two kilos of water-root was a damn good deal for me, given I had little in the way of drachma. I considered trading my now useless metafora compass, so that someone else could take their three turns with it, but I couldn't bring myself to part with it. I wasn't really sure why, but something made me want to hang onto the little bronze compass.

Plus, there was nothing in the market that matched it in value, so it would have been wasted financially.

I knew I had to get back to the bakery and start turning my haul into something useful, but I found myself heading toward the dome edge instead. The town I had grown up in was connected to six other domes, and there was a tunnel to each. As a child, I used to stand inside one of the tunnels as Lily zoomed around it in the water beyond, creating rings of bubbles that swirled around the clear tube like a watery tornado. I'd loved it.

I stopped when I reached the tunnel to the next dome. Either side of it were small pools of water that butted up against the dome edge. A woman lowered herself into one of the pools, and I watched wistfully as her legs morphed into a shining tail. I would have known she was a mermaid before I saw her legs change to a tail because of her blue skin and white hair. All merpeople had either jet black or snowy white hair. Her clothes vanished as her body changed, then she dove under the water of the pool. Seconds later, she emerged outside the dome, and a figure closed the distance, swimming toward her. A guy with his own gleaming tail. They grasped hands, then headed toward the bright surface.

Pools like this one existed next to every tunnel in Aquarius and they were the only way to get through the dome and into the ocean beyond - the places where water met water. I stared hard at the pool, willing some dormant power to lurch up inside me and make me want to immerse myself.

But nothing happened. Just like it had never happened as a child. I liked water well enough. I enjoyed the weight-lessness, I enjoyed the refreshing feel of moving through the liquid. But it didn't call to me like I knew it was supposed to. At best, I would describe my feeling for the ocean as an awed respect.

I blew out a sigh and moved to the tunnel. Once inside, I laid my hands on the glass and closed my eyes, trying to call up my image of Lily. I hadn't seen the vibrant depiction of her in my mind since I had seen the real-life version: the colorless girl turning to stone, lifeless in a lonely room.

Maybe I was avoiding her deliberately, unwilling to face the guilt I felt for leaving her alone so long.

"I wish you were here, now, making bubble rings," I told her.

My heart gave a relieved little swoop when her image materialized in my head, smiling.

I will be, soon. If you can pull off this crazy plan of yours.

"I will. I have to."

How are you going to breathe underwater? That's going to be your biggest challenge.

"I've got water-root. And a bunch of other stuff I can turn into something useful."

Good. Get on with it then, instead of standing around in tunnels.

I laughed out loud as she gave me her sternest look. "Yeah. Good idea."

"Almi, please don't do this."

"Silos, I have to."

My old friend stared beseechingly at me as I stood in the doorway of the bakery. I had set up a tiny workshop in Lily's room and had worked around the clock to fashion what I needed.

And now, I was ready.

I mean, I had tested nothing, and had about sixty percent confidence in my work, but that was as ready as I was going to be. I didn't have time to do any more.

"I don't even know why I'm worrying," the big man said, shaking his head. "It's not like they're actually going to let you compete. You've not even lived in Aquarius, hell *Olympus*, for eight years. It's not like you're just going to be able to just walk up and enter one of the most lethal water-magic competitions in all the realms."

His eyes were flinty as he spoke, and fear squirmed my stomach at his words. But I jutted my chin out and planted my hands on my hips. "I'll take that as you wishing me luck," I said. "And I'll say hi to your dad for you if I see him."

I spun on my heel, trying to ooze confident defiance as I strode out of the bakery.

"Almi." I felt Silos' hand on my shoulder and paused. He turned me slowly to face him, the hardness gone from his brown eyes. "If by some unholy cockup you actually get into the Trials, please, please, survive."

Impulsively, I hugged him. "Of course I will. Look after Lily for me." Leaving her, so soon after getting back to her, was the hardest thing. But I didn't have a choice. This was all I could do to save her.

"Always. Do you want me to walk with you?"

I shook my head as I stepped back. "No, you have to open the bakery. I remember the way."

"Good luck."

"Thanks. I might need it."

43

CHAPTER 7

I underestimated how long it would take me to walk through the ten domes and tunnels I needed to reach my destination. The farther I got from my only friend, and Lily, the more my trepidation built. The enormous belt around my waist was comfortable, but heavy, and I could have done without using so much energy right before the swim I was going to have to make.

I'd had to make my belt myself because my old belt couldn't take the weight of so many pouches loaded on it. It would also hopefully keep Silos' shirt, which was much too big for me, from billowing up like a tent when I got in the water. Altogether, the oversized shirt, massive leather belt, shell necklace and blue scarf I'd used to tie my hair back made me look, and feel, a touch like a pirate. I decided to embrace the likeness.

"Let's go, me hearties," I muttered, as I walked along a paved path in a dome much wealthier than the market-town dome I had grown up in. The closer to the palace I got, the nicer the domes became, and this was the last one. The houses here were all made of the fancy white stone, instead of hard-packed sand, and some even had gardens. Grass was rare in Aquarius. The buildings were also more spread out, meaning that I could move between them. There, like a gleaming beacon in the big blue beyond, was Poseidon's palace. I was almost there.

The edge of the dome directly opposite the palace dome was lined with pools, every hundred meters or so. I walked to the one closest to me, and nerves made my stomach flutter as I looked between the pool and the palace in the distance. This pool was different from the smaller pools that flanked the tunnels in the other domes. It was three times as large, and white marble columns stood at the corners, vivid green ivy creeping up around them. Broad shiny tiles in matching marble edged the water.

Grateful that there was nobody else around, I took a deep breath, dug into one of my pouches, and took out one of the tiny capsules I'd made the night before. The water-root would serve two purposes—if I'd prepared it correctly. It should enable me to hold my breath for about fifteen minutes, and it should keep me from getting wet. I had been able to create a liquid that made anything I dipped into it waterproof, and that had been one thing that had been easy to test, so I was confident that my belongings would stay dry and safe. Hopefully, the water-root would do the same for my body.

I did one last inventory check of the pouches on my belt, knowing I was just procrastinating.

"Water-root capsules—check. Ink bombs—check." Those had been easy to make with the grenades the griffin had sold me. I had loaded half of them with magical ink that kept multiplying and acted like a glue underwater, and the other half with little pellets that zapped whatever they hit with a shock of electricity. Neither would make me look adept at water magic, or hurt anybody, but they were the best I could do.

"Elephant chip—check." It was my last one, and I hadn't had the heart to trade it at the market, although I couldn't imagine a use for it in Aquarius. "Book—check." A thin canvas bag I had spent a hefty chunk of my available funds on made everything that was put inside it weigh little more than a feather, and not much larger than one. I had nicknamed it the 'Tardis bag', and I had the book safely stowed inside it. "Sketchbook—check. Compass—check. Dagger—check." There was nothing magical about the little weapon, but when I'd seen it in the market stall, I had loved the tiny carvings of shells in the wooden handle, and it was priced low. A weapon of any sort seemed like a good idea.

I closed the last pouch, satisfied I had everything. Sadly, I had failed to find or create anything that would improve my ability to swim or move through the water. I would have to rely on my own pathetic athleticism to get me across the expanse to the palace. Hopefully before the water-root gave out. I closed my eyes and pulled my image of Lily up in my head. "I'm doing this," I told her. "Now."

Yes, you are. And you're going to ace it, she answered me, using one of my favorite American expressions and beaming at me.

"Damn straight I am."

I opened my eyes and stepped to the edge of the pool as I swallowed a water-root capsule. Before I could freak out, I lowered myself into the water.

The temperature was warm, and I was surprised how good it felt as I let go of the edge and let the liquid take my weight. I had avoided water in the human world. It reminded me too much of the world I had been snatched from.

I kicked my legs experimentally, pushing my arms wide. It felt good.

I took a breath, ducking my head underwater. I waited a moment, letting the initial wave of panic I felt at being submerged ebb away. I knew I wasn't supposed to feel panic at being underwater—I was a sea nymph. But I'd felt it my whole life, and today there was even more to be nervous of. I was going to Poseidon's palace. If he caught me, I would be sent straight back to the human world, or worse.

I halted the negative thoughts in their tracks, shaking my head a little under the water.

Time to go, Lily said in my head.

She was right.

I swam slowly to where the water met the edge of the dome and pushed my hand softly against the glass-like material. There was a tiny bit of resistance, then my fingers slipped through. Gathering my resolve, I kicked hard, and the rest of my body followed out into the ocean.

It was cooler than the pool. A lot cooler. I kicked my

legs and pushed with my arms, the shining palace fixed in my sights. It looked alarmingly far away.

I sang in my head, in an effort to stop my brain trying to convince me that it was too far to make in fifteen minutes. I wasn't even sure my fitness level could keep me moving for fifteen minutes. It was entirely possible that I would drown due to exhaustion before making it to the palace.

You've eaten all the high energy food you could get your hands on, you'll be fine, Lily told me, interrupting my song.

I sang louder in my head, trying to keep my pace steady. A claustrophobic feeling was nudging at my consciousness, the knowledge that I was under tons of water, with nothing but an endless black void beneath me terrifying if I let it get to me.

I didn't know how much time had passed but I knew I was starting to feel cold. I was vaguely aware of shapes moving in my peripheral vision, but it was all far in the distance, so I kept my focus squarely on the palace. *Count the towers,* Lily suggested. *It'll be a good distraction.*

The palace was massive. Truly huge. It looked like a castle had a baby with an ancient Greek temple. Spires and towers rose up from the main body of the structure, all at different heights and most topped with triangular, distinctly Grecian roofs. The towers themselves had columns running from the ground all the way up to the top, and I thought initially that the spaces between the columns were glass. But as I got closer, I could see that some were completely open. Others did have glass between them, making up the walls of circular rooms, but paintings moved across the glass. A tower near the back of the palace stretched so high that it penetrated the top of the dome and reached the surface of the ocean high above. The second highest tower was the central one, which was wider than the others and almost reached the dome roof. I was willing to be that was where Poseidon's throne room was.

As I got closer, I got a good view of the small cluster of buildings around the base of the palace, and I guessed they were guardhouses and workshops flanking massive gates made of glittering black stone. Courtyards with green lawns and neatly cropped trees and bushes filled the spaces between buildings.

A sharp burn in my chest snapped my attention inward.

The burn got stronger.

Oh, shit.

The water-root was wearing off.

I kicked harder, my leg muscles aching. I was only a few minutes away, but I was twenty feet too high. I angled down, the burn in my chest getting worse, and an irresistible urge to take a breath built inside me. I was only fifty feet from the dome. *I could make it.*

Something hard crashed into my side, and I cried out involuntarily as I went spinning through the water. I clutched wildly at my belt, my instincts forcing me to protect my trinkets.

When I was able to orient myself, I turned, treading water, trying to see what had hit me. It was taking all my effort not to take a breath in, my instincts all working against me.

Something was coming toward me through the water. Something a lot faster than me.

I dove toward the glowing gold of the dome but I was nowhere near the pool that would let me in. Trying to keep panic at bay, I swam as hard as my depleted energy would move me. The water around me plummeted in temperature, and I risked a look over my shoulder.

My mind blanked as fear engulfed me.

Shark. Shark. Shark.

The only word my mind was able to form echoed through my head as the predator powered through the ocean toward me.

The creature looked as though it were made from rotten liquid, black and deep red swirling together over the surface of its leathery skin, and its huge solid-black eyes fixed on me. It opened its mouth as it approached, revealing a second row of teeth even larger and sharper than the ones I'd first seen.

I scrabbled at my pouches, trying desperately to remember where the grenades were. Not that they would do anything against a beast this size.

My fingers fumbled, and I was unable to take my eyes from the shark.

I was going to die.

I was going to be eaten by a fucking demon shark.

I'm sorry, Lily.

There was a flash of something blue and white, moving through the water like lightning, and then the shark *exploded*. Red and black liquid cascaded through the water like some grotesque firework. My mouth opened involuntarily, and through my shock, I was dimly aware of my lungs betraying me. Cold water filled my mouth as I drew breath, then flowed down my throat.

Shit. The shark didn't get me, but I was going to drown.

A face appeared in front of me. A beautiful, fearsome face. A face I'd loathed for the last eight years.

The fury in Poseidon's intensely blue eyes was the last thing I saw before the world flashed white.

CHAPTER 8

y back slammed against something solid, and I felt rough hands turning me over. My chest heaved, and light blurred my vision completely as I was hauled up onto my hands and knees. Then I vomited.

I squeezed my stinging eyes closed as all the water I'd inhaled left my body, the disorientation and pain in my chest making it impossible to think straight. When I finally stopped retching, I sat back on my heels, wiping my eyes with the sleeve of my shirt and trying to make sense of what had just happened.

I looked around, my whole body shaking with exhaustion.

The palace. I was kneeling in front of the gates of the palace. Three guards stood along it, none of them human. In front of them was a woman dressed in a skin-tight blue leather bodysuit, her arms folded across her chest and about ten weapons strapped to various parts of herself. Her white hair was secured in a tight knot on top of her head, and she was staring down at me with what I thought was curiosity.

"What in the name of Zeus do you think you are doing?" growled a voice from behind me.

Slowly, I forced myself to my feet, before turning to face Poseidon. There was no way I was facing him on my knees.

Even if he had just saved my life.

Was that what had happened?

I swallowed as I saw him, my cocky bravado shriveling.

Holy hell, he was… *magnificent.*

The last time I'd seen him, I had been young and utterly uninterested in men or power.

Now though…. He was just as tall and broad, his white hair loose behind his shoulders. But he wasn't wearing the ocean-robe. He was shirtless. Leather straps and belts crisscrossed his muscular chest and held weapons similar to the woman's, and he had his own pair of tight blue leather pants. I forced my gaze to stay above his waist, angry with myself that I wanted to look at all. This was the person responsible for separating me from my sister for eight years. He was the reason I hadn't already found a cure for her.

Thinking of Lily focused me, and I finally found my voice. "Hello, husband."

"You are supposed to be in the mortal world," he snarled, as I heard the woman make a small noise of surprise.

My stomach constricted. He was going to send me back. One flick of his wrist, and I would be back there, unable to help Lily at all.

"I am *supposed* to be with my sister."

I thought I saw him flinch, but I was unsteady on my feet, and my vision was blurry. I couldn't trust much of what I saw.

He stepped closer, as if he knew I couldn't see him properly.

"Why are you here?"

I shrugged, the movement making me stumble. "Heard there was a competition on. I'm here to sign up."

His eyebrows raised, then his gaze intensified. "Why would you want to compete in the Poseidon Trials?"

I stared back at him, digging for an answer he might believe. "I thought if I could prove myself to you, that you might help me," I said eventually.

"I hid you for a reason," he said, his voice low as he stepped even closer to me. "I do not want proof of anything from you."

"You can't marry someone, and then hide them away!"

"So you're here to claim your rightful place as Queen of the Ocean?" he said, spreading his arms wide. "A mere girl who just *drowned*?"

"So you saved me, just to dump me in the mortal world again, where I can wait for my sister to die alone?" I loaded my words with as much venom as I could manage, but I was so weak now that my words were slurring slightly.

"You know why I saved you," he hissed, his voice low and quiet.

"The stupid fucking Oracle," I mumbled. I swayed on my feet, and the slight loss of balance gave me a jolt of shock. I straightened. "Don't send me back. Let me stay with Lily in Fyka."

I could find another way into the palace, to steal the ship. I *would* find another way.

Poseidon stared at me, and I stared back. The colors of the ocean swirled in his eyes, and a breeze carrying the scent of salt and ruffled past me. My vision rippled again, but this time, when it cleared, I gasped. All of the right side of his face was covered in pale gray stone, spreading across his jaw and down his neck.

"Your face..." I took a step toward him, reaching out with my hand without thinking. He moved back abruptly, his expression hardening.

"What about my face?" he barked.

"It's... turning to stone."

I heard another gasp, then the woman in the blue leather appeared, standing next to Poseidon. They looked at each other, before both pairs of eyes settled on me.

"Lily is turning to stone, too." My brain was fogging over, and frustration made me clench my fists. This was important. If both Poseidon and Lily were turning to stone...

"Take her into the palace," Poseidon said. "Before she collapses."

I blinked at the woman as she nodded. "The palace," I tried to repeat, but my mouth had stopped working properly, and a weird bubbly noise came out instead. My left knee gave out, and my other leg wasn't strong enough to take my weight. My ass hit the tiles beneath me with a painful thud, and everything went black for a moment when my torso followed.

"Too late," I heard the woman say, everything around me sounding tinny. "Sire, she shouldn't be able to see the stone."

"I know."

"Is... Is she truly your wife?"

"Take her inside, and make sure she is not recognizable for what she is."

"What is she?"

"The last of the Nereids."

CHAPTER 9

I woke up in a bed. A much, much nicer bed than I'd ever slept in before.

My brain was slow as I blinked around myself, pain lancing through my head as I moved. I was in some sort of chamber, a round room furnished as a bedroom. I struggled into a sitting position and found myself patting my waist. My heart lurched as I realized my belt was missing.

All the fogginess vanished as I scooted up the bed, looking left and right around the room.

"Looking for this?" I spun, the woman in blue leather holding up my belt with one eyebrow raised.

"That's mine."

She tossed it onto the bed, and I groped for it. Just as I started to open the pouches it occurred to me that I might want to check my belongings when I didn't have company. I forced myself to lie back on the pillows.

"Who are you?"

"I'm Poseidon's general. Galatea."

"Oh." I eyed the myriad weapons about her person. I

had no doubt she could use every one of them. Her stern face was beautiful, and her gaze held a distinct 'don't fuck with me' edge. "Are you human?"

She snorted. "Of course not."

Eight years of living with humans caused a defensive flash of emotion inside me. "What's wrong with humans?" I scowled at her.

"Nothing, unless you live half a mile underwater and command the largest ocean army in Olympus."

I tilted my head in concession. She had a point. That would be tricky for a human. *Or a sea nymph with no damn power.* "What happened? Where am I?" I asked instead.

"I'm not sure what happened," she said quietly, her eyes appraising. "As for where you are, you're in the guest wing."

"Of the palace?"

"Yes."

I swallowed before asking my next question and noticed that my throat hurt like hell. "Where's Poseidon?"

"I have no idea. Now, this is not my usual job, but I have been tasked with making you look..." She trailed off and gave me another pointed once-over. "Different."

Snippets of the conversation I'd heard before I'd passed out came back to me. "He's turning to stone," I said, the memory of Poseidon's face smacking into me hard. I gripped the sheets as urgency took me. "So is my sister."

"Get out of bed. We need to find you clothes that fit."

"Why is he turning to stone? He must be able to stop it. He's a god!" If Poseidon, one of the three strongest and most important gods in Olympus, needed to find a cure, then surely one would be found?

Galatea looked at me, then let out a long sigh. "I can tell you're going to be a pain in my ass."

I nodded. "It's possible."

"Fine. Nobody except me knows about the stone affliction. It should have been invisible to you."

"How come you can see it then?"

"I can't. Poseidon told me about it."

"Oh. Then why can I see it?"

"I don't know. Nor does the king. That is why you are here, in the guest wing, irritating me."

"Does he know how to stop it?"

Galatea looked at me like I was stupid. "Don't you think he would have by now, if he did?"

I sat back, more pain gripping my skull. "Good point. My head hurts." I rubbed my forehead, trying to straighten my thoughts. My hope was fast fading, fear replacing it. If even Poseidon couldn't stop the stone...

I closed my eyes and called up my image of Lily. Slowly, she shimmered into being, blocking some of the pain of the headache. She smiled, and my thumping heart slowed a little. *Plan A, Almi. Nothing is different. Steal the ship, find Atlantis.*

I nodded.

"What are you doing? Maybe I should get a medic..." Galatea's worried voice made me open my eyes.

"No, I'm fine. Just a little slow."

That earned me another look that left me in no doubt of what she thought of my mental capacity. I sighed and swung my legs over the edge of the bed. "To clarify, I'm not being sent back to the human realm?"

"No. You are not."

Relief thwacked me in the gut. Poseidon knew I was here, and he wasn't sending me back. This was a good thing. "And how long am I staying here in the palace?"

"Until the Poseidon Trials are over, and the king can work out what to do with you."

The Trials! I'd totally forgotten. "I... I don't have to compete in the Trials?"

Galatea snorted. "Compete? You drowned after fifteen minutes in the ocean. You wouldn't survive five minutes in the Poseidon Trials."

"It wasn't like I drowned randomly," I protested, fisting a hand on my hip as I stood up. "There was a demon shark involved."

"That demon shark is called a *sápia aíma* and there's a lot worse than that in the Trials."

"It's called a what?"

"Rotblood."

"Well," I said. "You can tell Poseidon from me that these rotbloods shouldn't attack his visitors. It's rude."

I expected a sarcastic response, but her face tightened. "They should be nowhere near this close to the palace, or the city," she muttered. Her eyes found mine again, and she tilted her head. "You're really his wife," she said. It wasn't a question. More of a statement of disbelief.

"Yeah, if you can call a few words in front of Hera, then packing me off to another world to spend nearly a decade alone, a marriage."

Something in her eyes softened for a split second. "He tells me everything. But I didn't know about you."

I held my hands up. "Look, if you two are a thing-" She cut me off with a face that I didn't expect to see on one as stern as hers. It looked like she'd swallowed a slug.

"Poseidon is like a brother to me. I can't think of anything worse than engaging in... *sexual congress* with him."

"Huh. Well, I wouldn't know about *sexual congress* with him either."

"He never took you to his bed?"

"He took me to an altar, then to the Californian coast, and he left me there. Absolutely no beds involved." Something I had been grateful for. The man may have ruined my life and taken me away from my sister, but he never took anything more from me.

Galatea regarded me a moment longer. She had eyes that gave me the feeling that she knew exactly what I was thinking. They were such a pale blue they almost looked silver, and I found myself studying them so deeply that when she coughed, my cheeks flushed.

"Shall we?"

"Yes, right. Clothes, you said?" I replied in an embarrassed rush.

"Clothes. Are you wearing man's attire?"

"Yes. A friend gave them to me. My human clothes were drawing too much attention in Aquarius, and I have been away for eight years. I don't have anything here."

She rolled her eyes. "If you say 'eight years' again, there will be repercussions."

She shifted her weight, and a lethal-looking longsword skimmed her thigh in its scabbard.

I swallowed. "Well, I'm a touch bitter, but I'll do my best."

She left me alone to get ready, and the second she was gone I checked the contents of my pouches. Pulling out the Tardis-bag, I tipped out the book and my sketchbook, heaving a sigh of relief to see they were both safe and dry.

Flipping open the little book of memories, I ran my fingers over the pages as my mind tumbled through thoughts, one image dominating them all.

Poseidon.

I had seen him, fierce and furious, for the first time since that awful day.

My eyes focused on the sketches, my fingers turning the pages inexorably to the sketch I avoided the most.

I pressed my hand to the tear-stained drawing of my sister's bedroom, a shattered mug on the ground and a bad representation of me on my knees.

The image heated, and then I was back there, seeing the room as my eighteen-year-old self, taking my sister a coffee on the morning that was supposed to be her wedding day.

She was lying in her bed, her eyes closed, and I knew something was wrong instantly.

"Lily?" I dropped the mug and rushed to her, gasping as I touched her skin. It was ice cold.

"Lily!" My voice grew frantic. There was no breath coming from her lips. "Lily! Lily, please!" I dropped my head to her chest, desperate tears flooding from my eyes as I strained to hear a heartbeat.

Nothing. I could hear nothing. A wild sob burst from my chest as I clutched my sister, dizziness swamping me. This couldn't be happening. Lily couldn't be dead, she just *couldn't*.

A blinding flash of white light made me cry out, and the smell of the ocean crashed over me. I tried to turn, but my arms wouldn't release Lily.

I felt Poseidon's massive, godly presence, and then I was being pulled backwards, away from my sister. He cursed as he reached down, touching Lily's arm and recoiling.

"Leave her alone!" I yelled the command through my sobs, scrabbling back to her side. In my grief, I had no care at all for who I was shouting at. The almighty god could have done anything to me at that point, and I wouldn't have cared. Lily's lifeless form was all I could see, all I could think about.

Poseidon looked at me, his eyes filled with anger, then he clapped his hands. "Oracle! Explain yourself!" he bellowed.

A lyrical female voice filled the room. "The Nereid will sleep until the gods weep."

"What?" I stared up at Poseidon, and everything seeming to still around me, even my sobs. "Sleep?"

"Fucking deities," Poseidon hissed.

"She's asleep?" I said louder.

"Yes." Relief thumped through me so hard I felt my body sag.

She was alive. Lily was still alive.

Poseidon reached out, grabbing my elbow and I yelped, slapping at his hand.

"What are you doing?"

"We must marry. Now."

My relief that Lily was alive was momentarily halted as my mouth fell open. "What? Are you serious?"

"Deadly." He yanked me up to my feet and began to march me toward the door of my house.

"Let me go! We need to help my sister!"

"She is beyond your help."

A loud knock at the door pulled me from the memory, and I took a shuddering breath as the alien bedroom came back into focus around me.

A tear rolled down my cheek, and I brushed it away as Galatea's voice carried through the door to me.

"Are you nearly ready?"

"No!" I sucked in another shaky breath as I stared down at the book.

"I'm going to do this, Lily," I whispered. "He knows I'm here and hasn't sent me back."

You've got this, Lily answered in my head.

"I have. I'll let them reclothe me, and hopefully feed me, and then as soon as they leave me alone, I'll find out where he keeps his ship." Nodding firmly to myself, I closed the book and stood up. "I've fucking got this."

CHAPTER 10

I followed Galatea down a corridor that had columns along each wall and beautiful gold patterns forming crashing waves between them. I reached out, running my hand along the wall to see if it was paint or magic. The gold waves moved as my fingers skimmed them, and the smell of the ocean washed over me. I couldn't help the grin that sprang to my lips.

My little cry-slash-pep-talk had helped, the emotion caused by seeing Poseidon's face for the first time since I thought I'd lost Lily forever, now forging into hardcore determination. *I was in the palace.* Which was exactly where I wanted to be.

When Galatea turned through an archway and pushed open a door, I risked asking her a question.

"So, what is Poseidon planning to do about the stone thing?"

She looked sharply over her shoulder at me as we entered a new room. "Do not speak of it when we are not in private chambers," she hissed. I looked around, seeing nobody. We were in a giant dressing room, mirrors and benches and marble countertops lining all sides of the room except one, which appeared to be a mammoth walk-in closet.

"There's nobody here-" I started to say, but she whirled to face me, her face fierce.

"You will not endanger the King's privacy," she spat. I did my best not to shrink back from her, but she emanated so much anger it was hard.

"Okay. I got it," I said, holding my hands up.

"You will have a chance to talk to him directly about it, in circumstances of his choosing. After the trials."

"Circumstances of his choosing," I repeated. Geez, he sounded high maintenance.

"He is the King. And a god. It is his way, or no way."

"Ideal husband material," I muttered under my breath sarcastically.

"As I am sure you are perfect wife material," she said, cocking an arched brow.

"I never wanted to be a wife!"

She rocked back on her heels, then pointed at one of the benches. "Sit. Wait. The nymphs will be in to attend to you shortly. Do not tell them who or what you are. You will have your skin altered to lose its shine, and your hair will need to change color."

"My skin?" I asked. My skin used to have a slight shine, nothing on my sister's mother-of-pearl glow, but it hadn't shone since I was in the human world. And my hair was brown.

She pointed again at the bench. "Sit. Wait. Don't speak to anyone."

SECRET OF THE BROKEN KING

I did as she told me, and my breath caught as I saw my reflection in the ornate dresser mirror.

My hair was the tiniest bit blue. Powder blue. And my skin did have a slight shine, like when I'd been a kid. I pulled at the neck of my shirt and looked down at my tattoo, almost scared to breathe.

Please, please, let it have some color.

Nothing. A black outline of a nautilus shell, nothing more.

When I looked back at my reflection, my face was screwed up in disappointment and Galatea was frowning at me, amusement in her eyes.

"Why did you just inspect your bosom?"

I snorted a laugh at the word 'bosom'. "That's my business, thank you very much," I told her.

"You are very odd. I can understand why Poseidon did not keep you in the palace."

Anger bubbled through me. "He sent me away because he's an asshole, not because I'm odd."

Her face blanched. "You blaspheme."

"It's the truth. He didn't know me for more than five minutes. He couldn't have known how odd I was. He married me because of my species and that stupid fucking prophecy, then dumped me where nobody knew about me, so that he could live the life of a single man. I may be odd, but I'm not taking the blame for him being a prick."

"You should watch your mouth." The dangerous glint was back in her eyes, and I was almost relieved when the tangy smell of the ocean washed through the room, and the god himself's voice rang out after it.

"Galatea, I need you in my throne room." The words boomed through the walls.

She glared at me a minute, then spun on her heel, slamming the door behind her.

I turned back to the mirror, seething. A ripple of fear that the god had magically heard me calling him a prick and an asshole assailed my gut.

He didn't send you away because you're odd, Lily's voice sounded in my head. Her vivid image sprang to life as self-doubt flooded me.

"I *am* odd, though."

She laughed. *Yes, you are. In all the best ways.*

"Why did he send me away?"

So nobody could take you from him. Remember the prophecy? He who possesses the heart of a Nereid possesses the heart of the ocean.

I'd been over this with Lily lots of times in my head and drew the same conclusion now that I always had. "It doesn't even make sense. Firstly, what is the heart of the ocean? And secondly, I'm not even a proper Nereid."

Lily frowned. *You are a proper Nereid.*

Before I could respond, the door behind me pushed open. Two nymphs came in, their skin the same powder blue as my hair and their robes gleaming white.

"Hello. We're here to make sure you fit in at court and look like a human," the smaller one said with a shy smile.

"Great," I replied. "Is there any chance this makeover comes with food?"

It turned out the makeover *did* come with food. A huge tray of fruit and pies and cold meat cuts followed swiftly after the nymphs. I devoured everything I could as they covered me in magical powders and did strange things to my hair. I gave up watching them in the mirror after a while, instead using the time to work out my plan.

I would go along with everything I was told to do, I decided. The less of a pain in the ass I was, the more likely it was they would leave me alone. I didn't know how long the Trials would take. I was guessing maybe a week? And they should keep both Poseidon and Galatea busy.

"Are all the competitors in the Trials staying in the palace?" I asked the nymph who was covering my hair in some sort of shiny goo.

They grinned back at me, nodding enthusiastically. "Yes. It's been so interesting working on so many different species."

That was good. If there were a number of strangers staying in the palace that would only make it easier to roam about. I decided to try my luck.

"Did any arrive on ships?"

"I'm sorry, I don't know. Please close your eyes, so we can do your make-up."

I did as they asked, sinking back into my thoughts. One doubt was starting to surface from the rest, and I was struggling to ignore it. If the book was to be believed, then Poseidon knew about Atlantis, and the Font of Zoi. And if that was the case, why hadn't he used it himself to cure his stone affliction?

He hadn't fallen into a magical coma before turning to

stone like Lily had. Were they the same sickness? Or did Lily now have two things I needed to fix?

If the Font of Zoi was as powerful as the book insinuated, then it should deal with both the sleep and stone. Which meant it wasn't worth waiting until after the Trials to see what Poseidon was planning to do about his own problem. I would be best off getting the hell out of the palace as soon as I could—before he could change his mind and send me away again.

"We've picked some outfits for you for the ceremony tonight, and your hair and make-up is all done," said the small nymph. I snapped my eyes open and saw the taller nymph standing in front of the closet, two dresses hanging on either side of the doors.

"Whoa," I breathed.

I had never owned a dress. Not because I didn't like them, but because they were impractical for somebody who rummaged through trash or stole things regularly.

But if I *were* to ever own a dress, then the two in front of me were beyond what I could have hoped for. They were utterly gorgeous.

One was an inky blue, with a huge, puffy bottom half and long drapey sleeves. The other was much slimmer fitting, a pale green satin with a plunging neckline, and an even lower back.

"Erm, which do you like best?" I asked, looking between the two nymphs.

"Your frame is very slight, and the paler dress may suit a more voluptuous silhouette," the smaller nymph answered thoughtfully.

A polite way of saying I needed to get some weight on my bones, I thought. "Let's go with the dark blue one."

"What's your name?" I asked, as they helped me into the surprisingly heavy dress. It had a corseted bodice, and it took both of the nymphs to help pull it tight.

"I'm Mov, and that's Roz."

"I'm Almi."

"We know. Are you ready to see yourself?"

"Sure."

My casual response didn't match my face when Roz slid a door across to reveal a full length mirror.

My jaw fell open.

I looked nothing like myself. I mean, my deep green eyes were the same, and my nose and mouth didn't look much different. But other than that... My once-pale skin was tanned, as though I'd spent a lot of time out in the sun. The make-up on my face made me look older, more distinguished. Perhaps even... Pretty. But the biggest difference was my hair. Mousy brown and shoulder-length, my hair usually spent its time tied out of my way in a knot on top of my head. But now, long strands fell in soft waves all about my face, the bulk of it in a complicated braided updo. The updo wasn't what was making me gape though. It was the color.

"My hair is purple."

"More of a lavender, I think," Mov said. "It is a very popular color in court right now. You look like a human wanting to be a part of Aquarius elite." They gave a satisfied nod of their head.

I turned to the side, trying to see more of it. There

were strands of blue and mauve and lavender, weaving all throughout.

"I love it."

"You do?" Mov looked pleased.

"I really do. I look like a movie star." I did a little twirl in the dress, making the full skirt poof out. A small panic shot through me though as I faced the mirror again.

My tattoo.

It should have been visible above the sweetheart neckline of the corset, but I couldn't see it in the reflection. I looked down at myself, relieved to see the shell outline below my sternum, the lines skimming my chest.

Not wanting to assume that the nymphs knew about my tattoo, or that it signified what I was, I said nothing. I would ask Galatea why I couldn't see it in the mirror when I next saw her. A scowl took my mouth as I thought of the stern general. I had to stop being so antagonistic to her. And to the almighty watery asshole.

As if on cue, the door to the dressing room banged open, and blue leather and white hair came into view.

Galatea gave me a quick look, then nodded. "You will fit in fine. Leave," she said to the nymphs. They both scurried off.

"Look, I just wanted to say sorry for being so-" I started to say, but she held up her hand.

"Poseidon has need of you."

"What? He's not needed me for..." I stopped speaking before saying *eight years,* dipping my eyes to her broadsword. I could have sworn she nearly smiled.

"You are to attend the Poseidon Trials ceremony tonight, under the guise of being a reporter."

"A reporter?"

"Yes. You have a large mouth and like asking questions. The persona should fit, and it is a valid reason for a human to be at such an event."

I deliberately kept my *large mouth* shut.

"Do not tell anybody who or what you really are. To everyone else, you are human. Poseidon has made sure your tattoo is invisible to all others. Nobody in the palace, other than the three of us, knows the truth. It must stay that way."

"You have made that abundantly clear," I said.

"Good."

"Can I keep my own name?"

"Yes."

"Can I call you Gala? Or Tea?"

She let out a long sigh. "No. You should not have to interact with Poseidon tonight, or indeed throughout the Trials. Stay out of trouble, and the next few days should pass uneventfully."

"Got it."

"Then we can find out why you can see the stone, when nobody else can. If you have designs on living as Poseidon's wife when this is over, with a crown and a place as Queen, then I'm afraid you may be disappointed." Her voice was surprisingly soft, and I got the impression she was telling me this not to be spiteful, but to manage my expectations.

It didn't stop the indignant defensiveness rising up through me like a firework. "You think I want to be a frigging Queen? Married to him?"

Her icy eyes bored into mine.

73

"Look, I don't need a man. When I cure my sister, I'll have all the company I need. I'm quite happy to stay well out of the way of his watery lordship." The truth was, he'd frightened the ever-living shit out of me the first time I'd seen him. The sooner I could get some distance between us, the better.

"I believe you," Galatea said eventually. "And I believe it must be difficult to be forced to marry against your will."

I froze, her words were so entirely unexpected. "Yes." Then I shrugged. "Well, being married to him is easy, actually. He's completely ignored me the entire time. What I objected to was being removed from my home." And Lily.

Galatea nodded. "Come. It is time to welcome the competitors."

I stepped forward, slightly off balance in the heavy dress. Again surprising me, she reached out an arm, steadying me.

"Thanks."

"Thank me by behaving yourself tonight," she said.

CHAPTER 11

I followed Galatea down more corridors decorated with the enchanting gold wave paintings, my mind bouncing between thoughts like some sort of ping pong game. I couldn't help myself imagining what it would actually be like to be a Queen, living in this much luxury. Living in the shitty circumstances I had for years, I had poured all of my concentration on getting back, and I'd never given any thought to the fact that I was technically a queen. I was a business transaction to Poseidon, nothing more, and that had been easy for me to accept.

There had been a period when I'd been interested in men, times when I had been lonely and my body made demands my head wasn't sure it wanted. But I'd never acted on them. Not through loyalty to Poseidon, but because I couldn't see what the point would have been. If I had found a man, been with him, fallen for him, even, what could I have done about it? Hera was goddess of marriage in Olympus, and her rules were clear. One partner. No more. I might have been able to bring a human lover back with me, but then what? I couldn't marry them. And I didn't know the ocean god, *my husband,* well enough to know if he would have ignored his wife having a lover.

No, I had accepted a life without love not long after my forced wedding vows. But I had never, ever accepted a life without my sister.

The sound of hooves clacking on tiles drew my attention back to reality, and I looked over my shoulder.

A centaur was moving down the corridor behind us, catching us up fast. She was wearing body armor on her human torso, crossbows hanging from her hips and knives strapped to her amor-clad chest. Her brown hair hung around her severe face in tight braids, and her powerful horse body had symbols shaved into the chestnut-colored hair. She was magnificent.

"Galatea," she nodded at the general as she passed us. Her tail was braided in the same way as her hair. Galatea nodded in return, and a wave of excitement swept over me. I really was back. Years of no magic, and now... centaurs in the corridors.

We turned into a wider hallway, with nothing but air between the columns, and pedestals displaying busts of fierce looking fighters of all species lining it. Many were sea creatures. The hallway sloped upward, and I looked out as we moved along it. We were moving between two towers, I realized, and in the distance was the endless blue of the ocean. Shapes moved in the water, too far away to make out.

Ornate white double doors stood at the end of the

hallway, and Galatea strode toward them. They swung open as we reached them, and a voice rang out.

"Welcome, Galatea of Aquarius, General of Poseidon's Armies." There was a small ripple of applause as she stepped into the room. I took a breath and followed her.

"Christ on a cracker," I mumbled. The room was circular, and I assumed it was a whole floor of the tower we had entered. Like the hallway, it had columns ringing it, holding up the ceiling, with open spaces between each one. But unlike the hallway, the view was not looking out over the rest of the palace and the ocean beyond. Instead, there was some sort of enchanted coral reef encircling the room. Color and life blossomed everywhere. Hundreds and hundreds of fish in every color and pattern I could possibly imagine flitted between enormous fans of pastel coral, and tall green sea grasses waved in the gentle currents as neon eels slithered amongst them. Streams of bubbles glittering with golden particles corkscrewed through the water like shooting stars. It was mesmerizing. So mesmerizing that I stopped in the doorway.

"Oh, sorry," I muttered, as someone bumped into my back. The woman just tutted at me, moving on before I could get a glimpse of her face.

I shook off my awe of the space and moved further inside. A nymph like the two who had dressed me appeared out of nowhere, offering up a tray of delicate glasses. Pale liquid bubbled inside them, and I hoped it was alcoholic as I swiped one up gratefully.

I tried to keep my focus on the other guests in the room, instead of the incredible surroundings, as I sipped at the delightful drink.

The centaur who had passed us was there, and so were two minotaurs, the bull creatures hulking and dark in a room where most of the guests were brightly dressed or blue-skinned. My gaze was pulled to figures without my will, and I guessed that those with the most presence were the Olympian gods themselves. As a child, I'd visited events where the gods had been presiding, but I'd never been this close to one. Other than the watery asshole, of course.

Without a doubt, the most-presence-in-the-room award would go to the god with black robes, silver eyes, and tendrils of smoke dancing over his skin. *Hades*. But I'd never seen him in human form before—he had always presented himself as an ethereal smoke-being in public when I lived in Olympus. I raised my eyebrows as I watched him from across the room, his mouth quirking into a smile as he conversed with the largest Minotaur and Galatea. Since when did the god of death go to parties and smile? He moved to the right, and I saw that a woman on his other side was holding his arm. She was dressed in a green gown, her long white hair braided with golden flowers. She gazed at him as though he were water in a desert, and I suddenly understood why Hades was smiling.

He'd found love.

I dragged my eyes from the couple, looking for more gods. Specifically, Zeus and Poseidon. They should have been oozing as much power as Hades. But I could see, nor sense, either. There was no furniture in the room, but small pools with large golden fountains decorated with horses and dolphins were scattered around, and most guests were clustered around them. I recognized Dionysus—his iconic leather pants, open Hawaiian shirt, and half-naked forest dryads draped all over him giving him away immediately. He was a party god, which I supposed was fitting for a god of wine. I could also see Athena, the snowy owl on her shoulder looking as serious as she was as she talked to a small woman with a headpiece with a crescent moon on it. Hera and Aphrodite were absent, but Apollo and his twin sister Artemis were together, talking quietly at one of the fountains. They both wore white robes, and had gleaming honey-colored hair.

As if sensing I was looking, Apollo turned to me. Even from twenty meters across the room, I felt his power as his bright gold eyes met mine. He smiled, and my insides flipped. He was beautiful. Male model beautiful. I forced away my gaze, taking a few steps in the opposite direction. I didn't want the attention of any more damn Olympians, thank you very much. I supposed I'd gotten lucky that Poseidon had such little interest in me, beyond owning me in marriage.

I realized I was stamping slightly as my thoughts darkened, and I relaxed my shoulders and softened my pace.

Take it all in. Learn what you can. Lily's voice sounded in my head, and I took a deep swig from my glass, emptying it. She was right. I was here to pull off a heist, and all and any information would be helpful.

There were creatures in the room I'd never even seen before, and I found myself doing my best not to ogle as I moved as casually as I could through the crowd. Something I thought might be a harpy was darting a shriveled hand into one of the fountains, and I moved closer to see that she was trying to catch the carp that were swimming in the pool. She was short, with torn leathery wings jutting from her back and folding around her shriveled body. Her face was misshapen and angry, her eyes predatory. I moved on quickly.

There were a lot of sea species present, and whilst I'd at least heard of them all, it was my first time seeing some. Most interesting to me was a creature that seemed to be made entirely of gray sea-foam. When I got close to it, I had an intense urge to throw myself into the ocean, and never again see the surface, so I decided to give it a wide berth, swallowing down my curiosity. I wished Galatea had stuck with me, just so I could ask her questions. But she was engaged in conversation every time I spotted her, and I had vowed to not make a nuisance of myself, so I was forced to stick to making my assumptions.

Just as I got close to a group of merpeople, all boasting skin in various shades of green through blue, and full heads of white or black hair, the announcer's voice rang out.

"Presenting Poseidon, God of the Sea, and King of the Ocean!" The smell of salty brine filled the air and I turned to face the center of the room, where a white glow was building. Guests clapped loudly as the bright light faded to reveal Poseidon.

CHAPTER 12

*H*e was wearing the robes I remembered
from that fateful day on the platform,
robes that looked like the ocean itself. His white hair was
braided back from his face, his broad shoulders tanned.
He looked like a Viking Adonis, and once again I cursed
myself for noticing. He raised the hand holding his trident
at the room in acknowledgement, but no smile came to
his lips. Slowly, his eyes scanned the room. When they
landed on me, they stopped.

My awareness of all the water in the room intensified,
and I heard waves crashing in the far distance. Galatea
strode up to him, causing him to look away from me, and
the feeling vanished.

I shook my head, gulping down fizzy liquid from my
refreshed glass. Why did he have such a damn effect
on me?

Seriously? Lily replied in my head. *He's a god.*

"Hmmm," I mumbled. "I'm not sure he has this effect
on everyone in the room."

"Why are you talking to yourself?"

I whirled at the deep voice, spilling my drink I was so startled.

Up close, Poseidon's presence was even more overwhelming, his eyes so intensely bright I couldn't look anywhere else. I dragged as much of my sass as I could muster to the forefront and jutted out my chin.

"Because I've been forced to live alone for years. There's been nobody else to talk to."

His expression tightened, and I found myself completely unable to imagine him wearing a smile. "So you talk to yourself?"

"I'm excellent company, thank you very much."

"Why are you here?"

"I already told you."

"You wished to prove yourself to me so that I might help you." His tone held no doubt that he didn't believe me.

I shifted uncomfortably. "This is your party—shouldn't you be talking to your guests?" I tore my eyes from his face and looked around us. Not another soul was looking our way. I cocked my head, surprised all eyes weren't on the host and the human nobody he was talking to, when I realized I was looking at everybody through a kind of shimmering film.

"We are in a bubble."

"A bubble?"

"Nobody can hear us. Or see us. So tell me. Why are you here?"

I didn't know if he was making a threat—his default

demeanor was so standoffish it was impossible to tell. "Galatea said to avoid you tonight."

Defying science, his mouth tightened even further. He looked like he was carved from stone. The thought made me realize something.

"I can't see the stone anymore," I half murmured.

"Never mind the stone. Why are you here? How did you get to Olympus?"

"Never mind the stone?" I repeated incredulously. "I thought that was the only reason you hadn't already sent me back to the human realm?"

"Gods, you anger me," he barked, and I took a step back as the rumble of thunder sounded. "Answer my question," he growled.

I folded my arms, trying to keep my rising fear at bay. His eyes flicked to my chest so briefly I almost missed it. Assuming he could see my tattoo, rather than assuming he was checking me out, I tried to weigh up my options.

I could either be meek and obedient and try to win his confidence. *Unlikely to work.* Meek wasn't really my go-to.

Or I could be so irritating he would get angry and leave me alone.

"You know, your trident is less impressive than I thought it would be," I said, as casually as I could. He looked at the trident, his eyebrows twitching.

I swear I saw actual waves in his eyes, silver foam speckling the bright blue. "You know, I could make you answer me," he hissed.

A true cold fear trickled through me at that. Could he force me to tell him the truth? Or worse, look inside my head?

"Yeah? Well, I could tell everyone who I really am. What would Olympus think of a king who married a woman against her will, then hid her from the world?"

"Olympus has low standards," he growled. "I highly doubt anyone would give a shit about who I marry."

"Do you?"

"Do I what?"

"Give a shit about who you married?"

The question tumbling from my lips surprised me as much as it did him. An awkward silence descended as he stared at me. The crashing waves in his irises had stopped, but his severe expression remained. "I must possess the heart of a Nereid," he said eventually.

An unexpected surge of emotion rose inside me. "And would you have dumped Lily in the human world, all alone, if you'd had the chance to marry her?"

"Yes."

"Why?"

"You are too valuable to be in this world, where anyone can see you," he snapped.

"Valuable? I'm not some fucking piece of jewelry!" I realized I was yelling and didn't have the self-control to stop. "What the hell is the heart of the ocean, anyway, and what the fuck does it have to do with me and Lily? Who the hell do you think you are, separating me from the only damn family I have left in the world, and leaving her to die alone!"

I hadn't even realized that I'd stepped forward until my finger jabbed hard into his solid chest. Pain lanced through my wrist, but it was too late. Nothing would stop the tirade of fury issuing from my mouth. The result of almost a decade of anger culminating in the discovery that if I'd got back any later, my sister might have been made of stone spewed forth, a tidal wave of hatred. "You're a monster! A goddamn asshole, with no compassion or kindness in a single bone in your body! You made me leave her!" I choked on the last words, heat burning at the back of my eyes and my whole body shaking. "You made me leave her." The sentence was a whisper this time, and a tear escaped, hot as it rolled down my cheek.

I jolted with shock as one of his hands gripped my shoulder. Fury burned in his eyes as he towered over me with a ferocity that made my entire body weak.

I'd fucked up.

I'd really fucked up. I'd taken my only chance at helping Lily and used it to yell and swear at the one person who would take me away from her again.

"You..." he said on a breath. His whole being seemed to swell, and more thunder rumbled in the distance. "You..." His grip tightened on my shoulder, and I sucked in a shuddery breath at the pain.

Letting go, he stepped back abruptly, and I stumbled. He whirled away, and the noise of the party slammed into me. I drew in deep breaths, dashing away the tears on my cheeks and not daring to take my eyes from the ocean god's back. He stopped striding across the room when he reached Galatea, snapping something at her. The smile vanished from her face as she turned to him.

"Are you okay? You look a bit... pale." I dragged my eyes from Poseidon to see the white-haired woman in the green gown who had been with Hades.

"I, erm…" I blinked at her. Adrenaline from losing my shit was coursing through me, and my legs felt wrong.

"Here," the woman said, and led me to a fountain. She sat down on the marble edge first, and I copied her, making sure Poseidon was still in my line of sight.

"I'm Persephone," the woman said. "Everyone here calls me Persy."

"Almi," I answered, flicking my eyes briefly to her.

"You know Poseidon, huh? Looks like he's giving Galatea a pretty rough dressing down." She had a knowing tone to her voice, and what I thought might have been a New York accent.

I finally focused on her. "Are you from the human world?"

"Yeah. Well, no. I was born here, banished for nearly thirty years, then came back." She shrugged and took a sip of her drink. "It worked out pretty well in the end though." She looked pointedly over at Hades. He looked like he was trying not to laugh at something a man with a red beard was saying.

"Thirty years?"

"Yup. I'm guessing you were not a spectator of the Hades Trials?"

I shook my head. She gave me a rueful smile. "Between you and me, these gods are messed up. But Poseidon? He's not as bad as everyone thinks he is."

My feelings must have been clear on my face, because she laughed. "Okay, so he *is* as grumpy as everyone says he is. But his heart is in the right place."

It was *my* damn heart Poseidon was interested in, I thought. *Possessing the heart of a nereid.*

His words came back to me. *You are too valuable.* The idea of me being or having anything of value to anyone was making my head spin.

I let out a long breath.

Why hadn't he sent me back? Why had he let me talk to him like that? I mean, everything I had said was true, and he totally deserved to be yelled at. But I couldn't believe I was still here, in the palace.

My eyes found his back again, and he stilled, as though he knew I was watching him.

"Are you from the human world?" Persephone asked gently.

"Yeah," I answered absently.

"Olympians, citizens, and all who are watching across Olympus!" Roared the announcer's voice.

All who were watching? So the Trials were being broadcast. That made sense, given that I was supposed to be masquerading as a reporter.

"Allow me to introduce you to your competitors!"

I couldn't see anyone that the voice seemed to belong to, but the double doors flew open. All the guests fell quiet and looked at the figures entering the room. Poseidon moved toward the door, Galatea flanking him.

A procession of four people strode in, coming to a stop in a line before the ocean god. I was unnervingly reminded of being one of the women lined up on the platform all those years ago.

Poseidon walked along the row of competitors, nodding at each of them. There was a good-looking older man with dark hair, pale skin, and leather armor, who could have been human by his appearance. Next to him was a woman with dark navy-blue skin, black braids, and a skimpy black robe. A lethal-looking spear was clutched in her hand, and her lips had a slight sneer to them. Next to her was a tall, ugly man with green skin, no hair, and a vaguely angry, vacant look on his face. Finally, there was a woman who looked... wrong. There was no other way to describe her. It was as though she didn't fit in her body somehow, her limbs slightly too long or short. She had the blue skin and white hair of a mermaid, but her eyes were dark and her whole body was twitchy. Poseidon paused when he reached her, his eyes narrowing.

After a short moment, he turned to the room. "The Poseidon Trials will commence at first light. Enjoy." With a brief, but piercing, glance at me, he turned on his heel and strode through the doors, his beautiful robe swishing with waves as he left.

Galatea threw a look at me, then hurried after him. Was that a look to say I should go with them? Or a look to say 'you've done quite enough already'?

"Well, I guess that's Poseidon in a good mood," laughed Persephone as she stood up. "If you'll excuse me." She gave me a sincere smile. "Enjoy the party."

I watched her swish toward Hades, his eyes shining with light as he saw her approach. A flash of emotion sparked in me, and I closed my eyes a second.

"Lily, help me. I need to get a grip," I murmured.

Yes, you do. I can't believe you yelled at him like that, Almi.

"I know. But, for some reason, we're still here. And he made the stone go away."

I'd been so caught up in my anger, I'd forgotten. The stone hadn't been taking over his face. Did he have some kind of magic, or cure, that could keep the stone at bay? If so, I needed some. If I could buy Lily any time at all, I would take it.

I looked around the room. All the guests had surged forward now to talk to the competitors. Nobody was looking at me. I set my glass down on the edge of the fountain, scooped up my skirt, and moved as quickly as I could toward the double doors.

CHAPTER 13

J hurried across the bridge-slash-corridor, not wanting to lose them, and almost shrieked in surprise when I reached the end and Galatea stepped out from behind one of the marble pillars.

"Jesus Christ on a cracker, what are you trying to do?" I gasped, clutching my chest.

"I could ask you the same question. Who is Jesus Christ?"

"A dude from the human world. I thought you wanted me to follow you," I lied.

"You're supposed to be a reporter. You should be interviewing the competitors."

"I don't want to. I want to know why I couldn't see the stone on Poseidon's face tonight."

Galatea sighed and rubbed a hand across her face. "Gods, give me strength."

I looked at her expectantly. "Does he know how to cure it?"

"No, or you wouldn't still be here," she half-growled.

"I'd tell you to ask him yourself, but given that you somehow managed to put him in the foulest mood I've seen him in for years during a five minute discussion, that might not be the best idea."

"Oh."

"What did you say to him?" she asked, then seemed to catch herself. "It's none of my business," she said, shaking her head and straightening.

"I don't mind you asking," I said, shrugging. "I told him his trident was underwhelming."

Galatea stared at me, and I couldn't tell if she was trying not to laugh, or trying to stop her eye twitch. "What the hell is wrong with you?"

"Nothing that couldn't be attributed to his royal highness," I smiled.

"You blame him for your apparent desire to anger everybody you come into contact with?"

"I blame him for a lot of things."

"Fine," she said. "I think it's probably best if I show you to your room."

I blinked. "But I want to talk to Poseidon about the stone."

"No. You're not talking to anyone else tonight."

I opened my mouth to protest, then closed it again. It might be wise not to push my luck with Poseidon tonight. He might even forget what I'd said to him and decide to be more helpful.

Yeah, and maybe I'll wake up tomorrow and have magical powers, I thought glumly. Fat chance of either of those things happening.

Still, going to my room was better. I would finally be left alone, and free to sneak out and explore the palace.

I followed Galatea, trying to keep track of the turns we were making. Eventually, we reached a plain white door, identical to most of the others we had passed, and she stopped.

"Here you are. I'll be back before first light to escort you to the Trials." She reached out and dropped something small into a hole in the door. Keys and locks in Olympus were usually orbs that fitted into holes. There was a click and the door opened to reveal the same bedroom that I had woken up in.

"Thanks," I said. She gestured toward the room. "Can I have the key?" I asked, holding out my hand.

My stomach sank as I saw her face tighten. "No."

"You can't lock me in."

"Yes, I can."

I felt like ice water was being poured over me. "So I'm a prisoner?"

"No, you are a guest. A guest who has no business being outside this room for the next six hours."

"I don't want to be trapped," I said through gritted teeth.

"You won't be. The palace is magical, if there is an emergency then the door will unlock."

I was certain I could hear reluctance in her voice, and I clung to it. "Galatea, please. I promise I won't leave the room, just please don't lock me in."

"I'm sorry, Almi." Gentle but firm, she gripped my shoulder and steered me into the bedroom. "I'll see you in a few hours."

The door closed behind her with a loud click.

The second she was gone, I tried pushing it. Unsurprisingly, it didn't move. "This is a fucking joke!" I bellowed at the door. It didn't make me feel any better.

"What the hell am I supposed to do now?" I threw myself down on the massive bed, trying not to notice how soft the sheets were.

You could sleep? Lily's voice was calm, quiet. The opposite of my raging brain.

"If I'd known they were going to lock me in, I would have stayed at the damn party," I snapped.

You've got days. Get some rest.

I snarled and got back to my feet. "I don't like being trapped in small spaces."

This isn't a small space. Calm down. Take a look.

She was right, I conceded, as I began to pace the room.

It was a massive bedroom. The ceiling glowed with a warm golden light that illuminated the whole space and made it cozy. The bed was in the center, under a window with blue and gold drapes drawn across it. My belt and all its pouches was exactly where I'd left it, on top of the excessive pile of pillows. A large bookcase with shelves full of books and trinkets stood against the wall on my right, and an even larger closet took up the rest of the wall. On the opposite wall was a door I assumed led to a bathroom and a dressing table, an ornate mirror perched atop it. I caught my reflection as I looked at it, startled by my elegant appearance.

I touched my purple hair, and felt my rage subside a little.

Maybe I did need a few hours to regroup. I could get

out of this crazy dress and take some time to think through everything that had happened.

I just needed some air. I glanced up at the window over the bed, then climbed up onto the mattress. Drawing back the drapes, I prayed it would open.

The view made my breath still for a beat. I could see the whole palace before me. The ocean around us was dark, making the golden glow of the dome even more beautiful. Spires and turrets and columns jutted up around the tower I was in, and I could see people moving along more walkway bridges like the one that had led to the party.

Remembering why I was at the window, I looked for a catch or handle. I didn't find one, but I did find a small depression in the center of the pane of glass. I pressed my hand to it curiously. With a small shimmer, the glass disappeared completely.

"Oh!" I pushed my arm warily out of the gap and felt a cool breeze blow across it. I leaned over, peering down, and vertigo made my gut swoop.

Climbing out the window was *not* an option. I was far too high up, and the tower wall below my window was sheer. That was probably why it wasn't locked. I retreated back into the room, leaving the drapes open.

With a deep breath, I moved to the dressing table, reaching up to pull free some of the pins that were keeping my hair back.

The purple strands tumbled around my shoulders as I sat down, and I realized I had been correct in thinking that I somehow had more hair than I did before. I couldn't help taking a moment to admire it. It was beautiful.

"Those nymphs know their shit," I mumbled, as I cast my eyes over the decorations on the grand mirror. The frame of the looking glass was made of the same marble that most of the palace seemed to be made from. Little sea creatures were carved into the stone, and I moved forward on the stool to see them better. There were ones I recognized from the human world, like turtles and dolphins, and the large starfish across the top corner. And there were more I recognized from Olympus, like the half-fish-half-horse hippocampus, and Charybdis the monstrous man-eating sea worm.

A breeze from the open window carried the smell of the sea into the room, and I inhaled deeply. I was home. I leaned forward, willing my connection to the sea to bring my magic to life like I had so many times before. I ran my fingers along the ocean creatures carved into the mirror.

"I am a creature of Aquarius, too," I whispered. "So why don't I feel like one?"

I felt something wet under my fingers and froze. Movement accompanied the moisture, and I snapped my hand back from the mirror.

"What the..."

My mouth fell open as the stone began to change color, the white marble turning a deep red where the starfish I had just touched was carved. Water dripped down the frame, pooling on the dresser below. I gasped as one of the arms of the starfish suddenly broke away from the frame. It wiggled a little, and then, with a squelching sound, the whole starfish came away, falling from the mirror.

CHAPTER 14

"Ouch!" said a voice as it landed on the dresser.

My heart pounded in my chest as I stared. None of the rest of the frame had changed, the other sea creatures still set in solid marble. But the red starfish...

There were more squelching sounds as it flopped about on the mahogany dresser.

"Did you just say ouch? Or have I finally lost it?" My voice came out a whisper, and the starfish froze.

"Erm..." The voice was high-pitched, and definitely coming from the starfish.

"Shit. You did! You just said ouch!"

"Well, you'd have said ouch if you fell on your face too."

I leaped to my feet, backing up from the dresser. The starfish continued to flop about, its suckers facing the ceiling.

"Could you at least turn me the right way up?" the high-pitched voice asked.

"What the hell is happening?" My legs were glued to

the ground as my mind raced through possibilities. Was the starfish a spy? Did all the ornaments in this palace come to freaking life?

"I don't know what's happening, because I'm upside-down," the voice replied. "I'd be much obliged if you'd turn me over."

Slowly, I moved back to the dresser and peered down at the beleaguered starfish. It was about the size of my palm. As quick as I could, I gripped the end of one of its arms and flipped it over. I heard its suckers grip the table as I snatched my hand back.

"That's better. Thanks."

"You're welcome. Who are you, and why are you in my room?"

"Ah, I was hoping you could tell me that. In fact, I have a number of questions."

I took a few deep breaths. "Shall we start with names? I'm Almi."

"I have no idea what my name is," the voice answered me. "I don't even know how I got here."

"You were on my mirror. Then all of a sudden you... came to life."

"How strange," the voice squeaked.

"Strange doesn't come close," I muttered. Although I had been away from magic long enough that I supposed I wasn't really qualified to judge. "What *do* you know about yourself?"

"I know that I am not a fearsome warrior." The voice sounded proud, and the starfish squished about on the wood of the dresser.

"Okay. Not a fearsome warrior." Given that he was

squishy and small, that was hardly a surprise. "Anything else?"

"I am male, and very clever."

"Clever, huh?"

"At hiding from my foes."

"Clever at hiding?" I frowned. "Were you maybe hiding on my mirror then? From your... foes?" I suggested.

"I have no idea. But that sounds likely." I moved closer, and he stilled. "You are large."

"I'm normal-sized," I protested.

"You are not human." It wasn't a question, and I raised my eyebrows.

"How do you know that?"

His middle raised a little, as though he was shrugging. "No idea. Can I touch you?"

"Ew, no!"

All of his arms bristled. "Rude," he said.

"Sorry, I just... you look slimy."

"I think, as I'm not underwater, I need the slime to breathe."

"Right. Why do you want to touch me?"

"I am compelled."

"By what?"

"My entire being."

I rubbed my hand across my forehead, staring down at the starfish. "I wish you had a face. I feel like I could trust you more if you had a face."

"Why wouldn't you trust me?"

"I'm the captive of a god, and I'm worried you're his spy," I admitted.

The starfish shuddered. "Captive of a god? That sounds dangerous. Perhaps we should hide."

I shook my head. "Any ideas, Lily?"

My sister's image formed in my head. *Let him touch you.*

"Why?"

He's cute.

"Who are you talking to?" the starfish asked me.

"Myself. Well, my sister. Except she's been asleep for a long time, so I'm pretty sure it's only my imagination really."

The starfish stilled, then his legs rippled again. "What is her advice?"

I closed my eyes, steeled myself, then laid my hand on the dresser, palm up. Opening my eyes, I spoke. "She says I should trust you. Because you're cute."

"Cute? I thought I was slimy."

"I guess you can be cute and slimy."

Slowly, the starfish moved, each of his suckers making a little pop as they came off the wood, then sucking back down on the surface.

I screwed my eyes up as the first of his cold, wet arms touched my finger. Almost instantly though, the cold vanished. He wasn't slimy at all, and as he kept moving, I felt his tiny suckers on my skin like soft little whispers. There was something weirdly comforting about his presence once he had settled fully onto my hand.

"So?" I asked him, when he'd been silent for too long.

"I like you," he said.

I cocked my head. "Most people don't."

"I am not people."

"No. I guess you're not." One of his arms curled up toward my wrist, and a smile came unbidden to my lips. He felt warm and right somehow. "You know, you need a name."

"You must name me for my skills."

"Which are?"

"I told you. Hiding from my foes."

"Who are these foes?"

"I don't know yet. But when I do, I am confident I will be able to hide from them."

"Good." I dug about in my brain, trying to remember the correct ancient Olympian word for 'hide'. "Kryvo," I said, as the word came to me.

A pulse of warmth came from the little starfish, and his red color deepened for a moment.

"I like that very much."

"I'm glad."

I moved backward, sitting down on the bed and lifting my hand to look at him more closely. "How exactly do you hide? You don't move very quickly."

As I watched, his skin changed color, blending seamlessly with my own. Gaping, I lifted my hand, turning it cautiously upside-down. Kryvo clung to me, completely camouflaged. If a person didn't know he was there, there was no way he would have been spotted.

"Wow. That's really cool." He flushed red again as I lowered my hand.

"If cool means good, then yes. I am clever at hiding. Also at seeing things in other places."

"Huh?"

"I am seeing things that I believe are through another starfish's eyes."

I leaned forward, lifting him closer to my face. "Like what?" Maybe he was meant to be a spy, but he'd hit his head and forgotten who he worked for?

"I can show you, but you need to trust me," he said.

Nerves skittered through me. "I don't mean to be rude, but I literally just met you."

"We are bonded."

"What? How?"

"I don't know. But I am sure I can show you what I see. I just need access."

"Access?"

"Yes. With your permission. It may hurt a little."

I leaned my head back, alarmed. "Hurt? You're tiny, how could you-" I broke off as a sharp pain zipped through my palm. "Ouch!"

"That is the level of pain I am referring to. Do I have your permission?"

"Well there's not much point asking after you've hurt me!" I protested. "You got stingers in those suckers?"

"Yes."

I stilled my hand, looking at him more warily.

"Would you like to see what the other starfish are seeing?"

I was about to say no, but curiosity got the better of me. Curiosity *always* got the better of me.

"Yes," I said begrudgingly.

More pain spiked through my hand, but not so intense that I did much more than flinch a little. I felt a weird rushing sensation through my arm, and just as I was thinking that the little shit had injected me with poison, my vision clouded over.

It cleared almost instantly, and a room came into view. Not my room, but one I had seen before.

Poseidon's throne room.

It was another round room, columns ringing the space. But it was so high up above the rest of the palace I could see the whole city of Aquarius in the distance, the hundreds of golden domes looking magnificent against the blue. It was brighter too, I guessed as it was closer to the surface, and where the sharp rays of light fell on the white marble it changed color to a shimmering pale blue.

The ceiling was domed and painted with a breath-taking ocean scene. A reef covered in sea-life was depicted, all the creatures I'd seen on the reef yesterday, combined with shadowy beasts that would haunt a person's nightmares.

A throne stood in the center of the room, shaped like an enormous cresting wave, and sitting in it, leaning forward and tense, was Poseidon.

"My king, if she can see the stone, then she must be of use to you," Galatea was saying from where she was standing before him.

"It is too dangerous to keep her here!" Poseidon snapped back at her. He was no longer in his ocean robe with his hair braided back. In fact, he looked as though he'd just been swimming. He was wearing his leather strapping, but his hair was wet and loose, and water glistened on his hulking chest. The angry control on his face was gone, and a different, very real emotion played freely across his features.

"I wish you would tell me why, sire."

"I have," he growled. "If others know the last of Nereids is here, then they may try to take her. Whoever owns her, owns the heart of the ocean."

"But sire… You married her, and you do not appear to own the heart of the ocean. If you did, you would be able to stop this blight."

Poseidon stood up, swiping at a bowl of fruit on the pedestal to his side. It clattered to the ground. "The prophecy was clear! I only had to marry her. I don't understand."

"If she has anything to do with our problems, we need to find out what. The rotbloods are attacking every day now. Our defenses grow weaker. If we lose trust in the palace's ability to expel enemies…" She trailed off as Poseidon's eyes snapped to hers.

"You felt it too?"

She nodded. "The competitors. At least two of them."

Poseidon raised an arm, sweeping his wet hair back, bicep bulging. "I had hoped I was being paranoid. I believe there is something amiss about all four of them. But the palace has not identified them as enemies."

Galatea coughed. "The palace has not been able to alert us to the sharks. Or keep the blight that ails you at bay."

Poseidon said nothing for a moment, striding out of my view. I heard his voice as he replied. "Tomorrow, after the first Trial, I will talk to her. About the stone blight."

Galatea let out a sigh of relief. "Good. Thank you, my king. Aquarius needs you."

I didn't hear all of Poseidon's reply as the vision faded, but I was sure I caught the words 'fucking miracle'.

. . .

I blinked repeatedly as my bedroom came back into focus, Kryvo bright red on my palm.

"I..." Raising my hand to bring the creature close to my face, I squinted at him. "Was that real?"

"Yes. I think I can see through the eyes of the other starfish statues in the palace."

I tried to marshal my tumbling thoughts. The way Poseidon and Galatea had talked about the palace suggested it had a magic of its own. Perhaps that was where Kryvo had come from?

"Were they talking about you?" the starfish asked me.

"Yes."

"Correct me if I'm wrong, but it sounded like you are married to the king of the ocean."

"Yes."

"Then why are you a captive? And why are you not with your husband?"

I scoffed at the word husband. As succinctly as I could, I filled in the starfish on the prophecy, what had happened to my sister, and my subsequent wedding and banishment.

"So why did you come back to the palace?"

I paused before answering him. If he was a spy, I couldn't tell him I was here to steal Poseidon's ship to reach a fabled realm buried at the bottom of the sea that might be able to heal Lily. "I wanted Poseidon's help," I lied.

"Given that you are married to him, I think he *should* help you," Kryvo said indignantly.

I couldn't help smiling. "Exactly."

"It sounds like being married to you isn't giving him this heart of the ocean though. Are you really the last of the Nereids?"

His question stung more than he could possibly have known it would. I swallowed. "I think the prophecy was probably talking about my sister. Not me."

I couldn't admit to him that I had no power. But that stolen glimpse of Poseidon and Galatea's conversation had confirmed everything I had suspected. I wasn't a Nereid. Or if I was, I truly was broken.

CHAPTER 15

J thought it would take me a long time to fall asleep, but I must have been more exhausted than I thought because I was out as soon as my head hit the overly fluffy pillows. Which I was thankful for when a loud knocking woke me up just four hours later.

I hauled myself out of bed, looking immediately for Kryvo. He was where I'd left him, on his own small pillow on the dresser. I moved to the door and opened it a crack. Galatea stood on the other side, hands on her hips.

"Get dressed," she said.

I gave her a salute, then slammed the door closed.

"Morning to you too," I grumbled, making my way to the closet and hoping there would be something suitable in there for me to wear.

"Good morning." The squeaky voice was Kryvo's, but it made me jump all the same.

"Hi."

I opened the closet doors and saw an array of clothing,

of two distinct types. Black, white, and brown utilitarian stuff, and ball gowns. I raised an eyebrow.

"Better not turn up to the first trial in a ballgown." Selecting black pants and a white shirt, I made my way into the bathroom.

"Where are we going?" asked Kryvo when I re-emerged clean and dressed.

"*We* aren't going anywhere. I have to go watch the start of the Trials." And then talk to Poseidon I thought, recalling the conversation I'd spied on him having.

I'd have been lying if I'd said I wasn't nervous to be around him. But any information at all on the stone ailment, or blight, as he had called it, could be important.

The fact that he must know about the healing font and hadn't used it nagged at me, but I was unwilling to give it ground in my mind. Mainly because, if I did, I had no plan at all, and I couldn't bear that.

"What are the Trials?"

"A deadly competition to see which of four powerful competitors is strong enough to be on Poseidon's personal guard."

"Oh yes, that doesn't sound appropriate for a starfish of my constitution," he said, arms rippling. "I'll stay here."

I cocked my head at him as I strapped on my belt. "You know, actually, you could be useful."

He stopped moving. "How so?"

"If I take you with me, you might be able to see things I can't. Or hear things I can't."

"No. I think I should hide. I mean, stay, here."

"Too late, buddy. You're coming with me. I'll clear you out a pouch."

107

He flushed a bright orange. "I am not getting in one of those pouches. If I am to go with you, I shall stay out in the open air, and hide using my superior skills."

"Okay," I shrugged. I stepped over to the dresser and tied my hair back from my face with my scarf. "Where do you want to go?"

I had left my shirt unbuttoned over my bandeau vest, and tucked into my belt. I rolled my sleeves up and showed him my forearms. "Left or right?"

"I will not feel safe on your fragile limbs." I frowned, but he carried on. "I will adhere myself to your collar."

"My collar?"

"Yes."

I looked down at my chest. He would fit between my shoulder and my collarbone, and still be able to see out. "Fine."

I picked him up, again getting a pleasant sense of rightness as I touched him. Carefully I placed him on my skin. I felt a tiny amount of pressure as he glued himself to me.

"You know how weird this is, right?"

"No."

I watched in the mirror as he rippled, then vanished. "I guess we're ready to go."

I half expected Galatea to look straight at the starfish and ask me what the hell it was doing there, but she just gave me a cursory glance when I opened the door and then strolled down the corridor. I hurried after her.

"I like your belt," she said.

I looked at her in surprise. "Oh. Thanks. I made it myself."

"Stay out of everyone's way, and Poseidon will see you after the Trial."

I remembered to look like I wasn't already aware of the sea god's plans. "He will?"

"Yes."

I followed Galatea all the way out of the palace to a grand courtyard stretching to the gated entrance.

I looked up, still in awe of the ocean above me after so long away from Aquarius. A pod of whales passed over the dome, their silhouettes dark against the bright light of the surface, and I grinned. We weaved our way through a maze of intricately pruned hedges and trees until people came into view, standing in front of the gates.

A row of Poseidon's guards, all with black or white hair and blue leather on, stood with spears at intervals along the entrance to the palace. In front of them stood the four competitors that had been introduced the night before. Along each side of the garden courtyard were the guests from the ball, Hades and Persephone included. Again, I scanned the faces for Zeus and Hera, or Aphrodite, but couldn't see them.

A crowd had gathered on the other side of the gates, clapping and whooping, presumably spectators from the rest of Aquarius and Olympus.

There was a flash of white light, and Poseidon appeared. He was dressed like his guards, and he held his trident aloft as everyone's gaze snapped to him.

"Welcome to the Poseidon Trials," he boomed. I scanned the four figures, looking for signs of cockiness or nerves. One of them would win this competition. Perhaps not all of them would survive it. I swallowed down the discomfort that made me feel.

Remembering what both Poseidon and Galatea had said during the conversation I wasn't supposed to have heard, I looked even harder at the competitors. The mermaid was the one that most made me agree with their suspicions that something was amiss about them. Something about her made me feel inexplicably uncomfortable.

"We shall start with a warm-up round. A short test of your abilities. The winner will gain an advantage over the other three," Poseidon said, pacing up and down the line of competitors.

The good-looking guy on the end stepped forward, and Poseidon paused.

"Your Majesty," the man said, bowing low.

An icy chill blew across my skin at his voice. It wasn't a normal voice. It rang with a deep, unmistakable power, though he hadn't spoken loudly.

Almost imperceptibly, Galatea drew her sword beside me.

"You dare interrupt me?" Poseidon said, facing the man.

"But I must interrupt you," he answered, straightening. He had a smile on his handsome face, and I saw something flicker in his eyes. "I'm afraid you are laboring under false pretenses, my king."

Poseidon took a step closer, fury dancing in his eyes.

Thunder rumbled in the distance. "Enlighten me," he growled.

"By all means. I must admit to a little… trickery." His eyes flashed again, and suddenly he was the same height as Poseidon. His dark leather armor vanished, replaced by gleaming silver straps that looked like liquid metal, tight over hulking muscle. His skin changed color, turning almost alabaster white, and his hair grew, changing to jet black as it fell down his back.

An emblem on the belt on his black pants surged with light. It was a globe, made up of interconnecting rings. I gasped, along with everyone else in the crowd. That emblem was famous. It was the emblem of the long-defeated Titan, Atlas.

Poseidon snarled and Hades appeared beside the ocean god in a flash of black smoke.

Atlas chuckled. "Ah, I see at least one of your brothers still stands by your side."

"Where have you been?" Hades said. "We presumed you dead after the Titanomachy."

Memories of my sister telling me all about the war Zeus and the Olympians waged against the ancient Titans skipped through my mind.

"You presumed wrong. I was merely asleep. Until I was awakened by a most unexpected god." Atlas looked between Poseidon and Hades. "Your wayward brother."

"Lies! Zeus would never wake a Titan," Poseidon barked. But Hades looked less convinced.

"Well, he did. And he gave me a gift. The perfect way to exact revenge on the one god I despise with every fiber of my immortal being." His eyes flashed again as they bore into Poseidon. "Zeus had his beautiful wife, Hera, with him. You are aware of Hera's powers over marriage, yes?"

Poseidon froze.

"Of course," said Hades.

"It is time to pay for your sins, Poseidon," Atlas said, stepping close to the sea god. "You killed my wife. And now, I shall return the favor."

CHAPTER 16

*G*alatea stepped in front of me at the exact same time Poseidon's eyes flicked my way.

Atlas roared in triumph, and suddenly I was lifted from my feet, flying through the air. I bit back a shriek as I came to a halt, high above the crowd below.

"Your issue is with me, not her!" roared Poseidon. "Let her go!"

My heart was smashing against my chest, sweat instantly pouring from every damned cell in my body as I flailed in the air. *What the fuck was happening?*

"You want to save her?" I kicked and struggled as I floated toward the edge of the golden dome. My panicked mind faltered as I saw what was beyond the dome.

Six rotbloods, lined up, their onyx eyes fixed on me.

"Let her go!"

"I want control of the Trials. And the prize is no longer to be part of your pitiful army. The prize is your trident. Your realm. Your crown."

Bile rose in my throat as I got closer to the dome edge, fear making my skin feel like ice. I was vaguely aware of a pain in my shoulder, and the slight squeak of Kryvo's voice, but my blood was pounding too loud in my ears to concentrate.

The only words filtering through were those of the gods below me.

I was going to die.

There was no way in Olympus that Poseidon would give up his trident, realm, and crown to save me.

"Can I compete?" Poseidon's voice was granite, and I was so shocked that my limbs stopped flailing. I craned my neck, looking down.

"Of course. It would only be fair to give you a fighting chance at defending yourself." Atlas' voice was mocking, as though Poseidon didn't stand any such chance.

"I'll do it."

I could have sworn my heart actually stopped for a split second, then I was tumbling through clear air toward the marble. There was a flash of white, the strong smell of the ocean, and then I found myself on my ass at Galatea's feet. Fury lined every inch of her face, but I hardly saw her. My eyes went straight back to Poseidon.

"Excellent," beamed Atlas, rubbing his hands together. "Let me introduce you to your competition." He gestured at the three other competitors, and with a loud crack and shimmer, the woman transformed before my eyes.

I scrambled to my feet, feeling sick and dizzy as I tried to make sense of what was happening.

She looked nothing like she had just a few seconds ago.

About six feet tall, she was wearing a black gown that was a similar shape to the one I'd turned down due to my lack of curves. This woman had no such issues. She looked stunning in it, the fabric hanging from voluptuous hips and breasts, her dark skin glowing. But that wasn't what made her stand out. Her hair was made of water. I could see straight through it, and it moved when she stood still, swirling around her perfect face, her icy blue eyes seeming to glow the same hue.

"Kalypso, Titan goddess of water," Atlas boomed, gesturing to her. My stomach swooped. Kalypso? My sister had told me stories of the legendary water Titan. If they were to be believed, then she was as merciless as she was powerful. Looking at her cold eyes, I was inclined to believe.

The marble tiles rumbled beneath my feet, then the next man in the row shimmered and transformed.

"Polybotes, giant offspring of Gaia herself," Atlas grinned.

Twice the height of Kalypso and built like an oak tree, the giant stamped his feet, making the tiles rumble again. His face looked as though it had been beaten in times past and new, but his bright blue eyes were alert. And angry.

The shimmering started up again, and the mermaid began to change.

I held my breath as primal fear made me want to turn and run, far *far* away from the most terrifying creature I'd ever seen.

She had the torso of a woman, hulking with muscle, but the bottom half of an octopus. Tentacles slid across the courtyard tiles, covered not in suckers but thorny barbs. She was a deep red color, ripples of darker red and black moving constantly across the surface of her skin, making her look as though he was covered in liquid. Her eyes were like that of a shark, onyx black and unblinking, and she didn't have a hair on her skeletal head.

"Ceto, goddess of sea monsters."

Holy shit. Kids across the whole of Olympus had nightmares about this god. Hell, so did their parents. Just about every deadly creature in the ocean could call her their creator.

"And of course, for those who don't already know her, our final competitor, Almi! Last of the Nereids, and Poseidon's wife!"

My heart stuttered in my chest, and a new wave of dizziness stole my breath as every eye in the courtyard landed on me.

Every eye except Poseidon's. In a beat, he was at Atlas' throat, fingers wrapped around his neck. "We just made a deal," he snarled.

"Yes. I agreed not to feed her to the rotbloods. I never said anything else." Atlas' eyes were as hard as the sea god's. "I have thought about the woman you took from me every day for centuries. You will pay, Poseidon. You will feel the pain I have endured."

Poseidon bared his teeth and raised his trident. But it was as though his hand had got stuck in mud. He looked at his arm in confusion, then the trident floated up into the air. He let go of Atlas, reaching for his weapon, but it jerked out of his range.

Atlas laughed again. "Your prize!" he cried, pointing at

the trident and facing the row of hungry, lethal looking gods and monsters. "Control of everything Poseidon has. Yours for the taking."

CHAPTER 17

"*S*ee you in one hour to find out which of you will have the advantage."

There was a flash of light and Atlas was gone, and the trident with him.

Poseidon gave a roar of rage, slammed his foot down and whirled to face the competitors.

"You dare challenge me for my blood-earned realm?"

Kalypso shrugged as she stepped forward. "Blood means nothing in Olympus, Poseidon. If you believe the realm should be yours, you can earn it. Prove you are strong enough." She tilted her chin, swished her water-hair over her shoulder, then strode past him, back toward the palace.

Polybotes bared his teeth before he spoke, his voice uncomfortably deep. "She's right, Poseidon. You and I have history, and I intend to see you crushed." He slammed one fist into his other open palm, then stamped after Kalypso.

"And you? After everything I have bestowed upon you

and your brother, and after serving me loyally for centuries?" the ocean god said, turning to Ceto.

"You expect us to give up the opportunity to rule?" Her voice was an awful hiss, making me flinch. "I have as much right to compete as the others," she said. "And, mighty king, I have as much chance at winning."

Without another word she melted into thin air, leaving a murky cloud in her wake.

Beside me, Galatea moved, and I caught her arm. "What is happening?"

She glared at me. "You're about to compete with Poseidon, a Titan, a giant, and a sea monster for control of Aquarius."

"Why did Poseidon agree to this?" My voice was a whisper.

Before she could reply, Poseidon's voice rang out loudly, making us both turn. "Citizens of Olympus! It seems you will have a better show than anticipated. Fear not. I will smash these unworthy opponents into the depths and beyond. Atlas and his champions will be no threat to Aquarius." The gathered crowd roared as Poseidon raised his fists, his fierce eyes alive with passion. "I shall emerge from the Poseidon Trials as the undisputed ruler of the oceans." There were more cheers and whoops. "See you all in one hour!"

He clapped his hands together, and everything flashed white.

When the light faded I found myself in his throne room. And not alone. Galatea was still standing next to me, but Hades, Persephone, Athena and Apollo were all in a ring around the throne.

"Brother, how did Atlas enter your palace?" Hades asked immediately.

"Zeus must have helped him," Poseidon snapped back. He wasn't sitting in the throne but pacing in front of it.

"If Zeus is befriending Titans, we need to be worried."

Apollo nodded, and Athena spoke softly. "It sounds as though he has finally brought Hera over to his way of thinking."

"There is only so long she could fight her husband," said Hades tightly.

I tried to follow what they were saying, but my mind was racing, both with information and emotion.

It sounded like Zeus was no longer on the same side as the other Olympians, but that was so far down my list of things to worry about at that moment that I couldn't care less. I just wanted the other gods gone, so I could talk to Poseidon.

Persephone glanced at me, then spoke. "We did not know you were married, Poseidon."

Everyone except the sea god looked at me.

"No," was all he said.

Persephone coughed. "What did you do to Atlas' wife that has made him seek this revenge?"

I focused on Poseidon's face, desperate to know the answer to that question myself. But his eyes were cold, and his mouth tight.

"That business is my own."

"Brother, it might help—" Hades started, but Poseidon cut him off.

"I will not look weak, and I will not bow to the command of an asshole like Atlas. I will beat the others."

"And Almi?" Persephone's voice was harder now. "Forgive me," she said, turning to me. "I don't know anything about Nereids, but are you powerful enough to compete with gods as strong as those entered in these Trials?"

My skin seemed to tighten over my bones, and my ears began to ring loudly.

No, I wanted to scream. *No. I will die in five fucking seconds flat.*

Surely others knowing my secret was less lethal than continuing to pretend?

I opened my mouth to admit I wasn't, but Poseidon spoke first. "She will survive."

Persephone frowned. "But not win?"

"I will win!" He hit himself in the chest, and my eyes widened.

The stone was back.

It crept across his face, down his shoulder, and along his arm. My insides coiled with fear and doubt.

Poseidon was sick. Nobody else knew, but he was sick.

What if he couldn't win?

Much as I hated him, did he really deserve to lose his trident and realm?

What if that terrifying monster Ceto won? Or the cruel Kalypso?

Athena spoke again. "You have been challenged in public, and accepted. I believe that there is nothing for us to do now but see this through."

Hades growled and the temperature in the throne room rose. "This is part of Zeus' plan. He is using Atlas. We should not let this go ahead."

"That is precisely why we *should* let this go ahead. For too long, the king of the gods has been silent. It is time he made his move."

"And you would let Poseidon take the risk?"

"If we back Atlas, rather than fight him, then we should be able to maintain a measure of involvement throughout. With the Olympians supporting the Trials there will be less chance of cheating and lawlessness."

"I am willing," Poseidon said. He stood straighter, and the stone spread down his hip, out of sight under his pants. How could the other gods not see it?

Hades reached forward, clasping his arm. "Win, brother. Aquarius is rightfully yours—it can belong to no other."

"What will Atlas do if Poseidon does win?" asked Apollo.

"With any luck, he will call in Zeus," answered Athena. "And then we will have a chance to reason with our wayward king. Farewell." She nodded at the other gods in turn. "Win, Poseidon. Or great danger could befall the whole of Olympus." Then she vanished.

"No pressure," grinned Apollo, then he too vanished.

"Good luck, brother." Hades nodded, and Persephone looked over at me.

"If you need anything, let me know," she said, then nodded at Poseidon before they both left in a flash of white.

"Sire," Galatea said. "What—?"

"Please leave us."

She froze. After a painfully long pause, she said, "Yes, Sire," and whirled away to leave the room.

My body was so tense my muscles shook as Poseidon turned slowly to face me. He locked his eyes on mine.

"Why did you do that?" I blurted out.

"You need to stay out of my way. Just survive and let me take care of the rest," he said, his voice calmer than his wild eyes.

"Why did you give up your trident to save me?"

"You would have preferred I let you be fed to the sharks?" His being flashed with power, and a wave of weakness washed over me. His eyes softened instantly. "You need to sit."

A scraping sounded behind me, and I saw that a chair had been conjured up out of nowhere. I thought about protesting, but my weak knees got the better of me. I slumped backward, letting the cushions take my weight.

Scrubbing my hand across my face, I tried again. "Why did you give up your trident to stop Atlas killing me?"

Poseidon moved closer, his scent filling my nostrils. It was the ocean personified, fresh and bright and powerful. He opened his mouth, indecision shining in his eyes. With a snap, he closed it again and held out his arm. "You see this?"

"Stone," I answered. The gray granite moved with him.

"Not even the Olympians can see this. Yet you can."

"Is that why you saved me?"

"Amongst other reasons," he growled. "When the Trials are over, we need to fix it."

I held my hand up. "Wait. Firstly, what do you think I can do that you, an Olympian god, can't?" Fear made my gut clench at his admission that he couldn't fix it himself. That was seriously bad news.

"That is what I intend to discover."

I let out a long breath. "Right. Secondly, why are we waiting until the Trials are over to fix it? Is it not going to..." I tried to work out how to word my question without making him angry. "Slow you down a bit?"

His expression turned stormy, and he pulled his arm back. "No. *You* will slow me down," he snapped.

I leaned back, folding my arms. "I didn't ask for any of this shit."

"You came back! If you'd stayed out of the way, where I left you-"

"Then my sister would have died alone!" I shouted over him.

He stepped even closer to me, his own temper clearly on the brink. "Your sister is not the most important thing in Olympus."

"She is to me," I answered, stabbing my thumb at my chest.

Something flickered in his eyes, something that wasn't his dark temper.

He took a long breath and a cool breeze washed over my skin from nowhere. "You can barely stand up. This is not conducive to surviving.

I blinked at the rapid change of subject.

"You are malnourished."

"And who's fault is that?"

He clapped his hands together, and when he drew them apart he was holding a vial. "Drink this. It will give you enough energy to stay the hell out of my way and let me win this thing."

"I guess losing your trident hasn't made you lose any

of your charm," I mumbled as I took the magicked vial from him.

"Not true."

I raised my eyebrows as I sniffed the liquid in the vial. It smelled like woodsmoke and salt. "You never had any charm to begin with?"

"The trident is my connection with the creatures of the ocean." The anger had gone from his voice, and a tense sadness had replaced it. "It is how I charm them."

I looked at him as he gazed up at the ceiling, his eyes skimming over all the sea-life depicted there. "So... You can't control sea animals anymore?"

He shook his head, strands of his white hair falling along his hard jaw. "I can't even communicate with them, let alone control them."

"Does that include sea monsters?"

"Yes."

"Shit."

He looked back down at me, eyes bright and wild. "I concur."

"Huh. Nice we can agree on something."

"Drink," he said.

I did. The liquid tasted freaking amazing, like rich smoky tea. Warmth flooded my body, and I felt my muscles twitch. The tiredness drained away, and even my mind seemed more alert.

"That's good," I muttered. "Thank you."

"Just don't die," he scowled.

"I still don't understand why you care about my life so much."

"I have told you, repeatedly. I need to possess your

heart, as the prophecy foretold, and I need to find out if you have any connection to this cursed fucking stone blight."

I stopped myself from pointing out that possessing my heart was achieving nothing. I only knew that because I spied on his conversation with Galatea, and I had no intention of admitting that.

"What is the heart of the ocean?"

"Stop asking inane questions and leave."

"No. I have so many more questions."

"I don't care. Galatea!" He roared his generals name, and she strode through the doors to the throne room in seconds.

"Sire."

"Escort Almi to her room."

She looked pissed, but she nodded.

I didn't bother arguing. It was clear Poseidon was done talking, and besides, I could do with a few moments alone. I had a lot to process and talking it through with my imaginary sister in public might raise the wrong eyebrows.

"I didn't know that was going to happen," I said, as I followed Galatea down the corridors of the palace. Even her back seemed angry.

She didn't answer me.

"Honestly, I didn't know anything about Atlas, or even Zeus, I've been away so long."

Still no answer.

"What happened with Zeus and Hades and Poseidon?" I asked hopefully.

"They fell out. Olympus is paying the price," she spat.

"Oh?"

"Hades and Persephone, then Ares and Bella... Now Poseidon." She shook her head, then looked at me over her shoulder. "I'm not sure I trust you."

Weirdly, I appreciated her honesty. And frankly, she *shouldn't* trust me. "I didn't know that would happen," I repeated. "I didn't ask Poseidon to give up his trident."

She glared at me some more, then turned back. "The palace should have kept enemies out. *Someone* let Atlas in."

I couldn't help my snort. "And you think that was me?" It wasn't like I could tell her that I had no magic, but the idea was absurd all the same.

"You expect me to believe it is coincidence that your return and this mutiny occurred two damned days apart?"

"It is coincidence," I snapped. "Atlas is crashing your Trials, and I didn't set the dates for those—that was your king. How is the palace supposed to keep enemies out? Is it alive?" I asked, thinking of Kryvo coming to life on the mirror. I knew he was still hidden on my shoulder, because I could just feel his presence when I moved. I hoped he was okay.

"I am telling you nothing you might use against the king."

I sighed. "Fine."

We reached my room, and she opened the door with a little too much force.

"You locking me in again?"

"What do you think?"

CHAPTER 18

I went straight to the dresser when the door closed behind me, sitting on the stool.

"You okay, Kryvo?"

Alarmingly slowly, the little starfish turned red and visible again. I held my hand to my chest, and he inched his way off my collarbone and onto my palm.

"Hiding did not help me," he said quietly.

"Of course it did. Nobody saw you," I said, a very fake cheerfulness to my voice.

"If you had been fed to the rotbloods, they would have eaten me too."

"You could have detached yourself from me and swam invisibly through the ocean?" I suggested.

He paused in his slow shuffle to my hand. "That is a possibility."

"Good."

"Are you okay?"

His question caught me by surprise. "Oh. Erm, no, not really."

"I don't blame you," he answered. "You must compete with a Titan, a giant, a monstrous ancient sea god, and Poseidon himself in a series of lethal Trials. Can I offer you some advice?"

"I reckon I can guess what it will be."

"You should hide."

I nodded. "Much as I'd love to, I'm not sure Atlas will give me that option. It looks like I'm key to his revenge." I screwed my face up. "Why couldn't that fucking Oracle have picked a different sea nymph species? Why the hell do I have to be married to that tosser?"

"Do you wish him to lose the Trials?"

Kryvo was on my hand fully, so I lowered him onto the dresser. "I don't know. I haven't thought that far ahead, to be honest."

"You clearly hate him. Losing his trident and Aquarius would be apt punishment for someone who has treated you and your family so badly."

I cocked my head, thinking. "Lily? What do you think?"

Her image appeared in my mind. *Aquarius belongs to Poseidon. It should not be any other way. He and his brothers are the core Olympus is built on.*

"But he's miserable, and mean, and selfish and, well, just an asshole."

He is a fair ruler.

"Fair? What the hell is fair about what he has done to us?"

He separated us, but he never hurt us. Many gods would have done much worse.

I let out an angry snort. But as I let the thought roll

around in my head a little more, I began to wonder if she was right.

Not about Poseidon not being an asshole—that was *not* up for dispute. But about him being the right ruler of Aquarius. Atlas had some bad vibes going on. I realized I had assumed that whoever won would rule alongside him, but that may not be the case. I made a mental note to find out why Atlas wasn't competing himself, and considered the others. Kalypso was strong and powerful. She might make a good ruler. But the stories about her were all of a being with no mercy and an explosive temper. Polybotes the giant was unknown to me, so I couldn't guess what he would do as a ruler. But Ceto... The goddess of sea monsters and her brother, Phorkys the god of the deep, had created most of the worst monsters of the ocean. They scared me just to look at. I didn't want to think about what they would turn Aquarius into if they ruled.

"Kalypso is very powerful," Kryvo said, surprising me.

"You know her?"

"No. But there are paintings in the palace that tell stories. Where there are statues, I can see them. I shall show you."

I moved back to the dresser and picked him up, carefully setting him back on my collarbone. "You comfy there?" I asked him.

"As comfortable as I can be. Although I'm not sure being able to see out is very pleasant, given what you are about to face."

"Don't remind me."

The more I thought about what I was actually going to have to do, the more I felt like I was going to throw up.

Compete with gods in lethal Trials. What would be involved? I remembered what Silos had told me about people dying in the last Trials, and images of underwater cages and enormous, vicious sea monsters floated through my mind. My stomach flipped and flopped, apparently doing everything possible to make me feel more unsettled.

"Ready?" Kryvo said.

"Yup."

His little stingers attached to my skin, causing a sharp sensation that faded quickly, then the vision came to me.

Like last time, I was looking out from what I guessed was a statue in the palace. But instead of looking at Poseidon's throne room, this time, I was looking at a mural on a wall. All in different hues of blue, except for the sweeping highlights of gold, the painting was breathtaking.

It showed Kalypso fighting Zeus. She looked furious, her watery hair a whirlpool of fury matched by her eyes as she raised her arms, tidal waves rising behind her in response. Zeus was above her, clouds swirling around him, eyes electric and lightning bolts streaming from his fingertips, lancing through Kalypso's defenses.

The vision faded and I let out a long breath. "I don't believe the other Olympians would let anything that bad happen," I said, false hope in my voice. "So let's not worry about that. I just need to concentrate on staying alive."

I stood up and began rummaging through my pouches. I got out my water-root, and reloaded my stash in the top of one pouch so that I could access it more quickly if I needed to.

The vial had indeed restored my energy, all the tired, shaky limb problems I'd had earlier gone. I was sure I could swim for fifteen or twenty minutes.

"This isn't an actual Trial," I told myself as I checked my little grenades for the hundredth time.

Exactly. Just a test, Poseidon called it. A test you'll ace, Lily said in my head.

"Just a test. I'll be fine."

I felt sick.

A male voice sounded in my head, making me cry out in surprise. "Be ready in one minute."

It was Atlas' voice, and he sounded like he could barely contain his glee. I hurried to my belt, strapping it tightly to myself as my pulse ramped up a few notches.

"You staying there, or do you want to wait here on the dresser?" I asked Kryvo, secretly praying he would come with me. I didn't know if he could help in any way, but trepidation was causing fresh sweat to run down between my shoulder blades, and not being completely alone was appealing.

He paused before answering. "Are you sure you can't hide?"

"Quite sure."

"Then I suppose I shall have to come with you."

"Thanks, Kryvo."

I barely got the words out before the world flashed white.

CHAPTER 19

I found myself in a golden dome under the sea dominated by a single structure. An arena.

Oval in shape, it reminded me of a coliseum, except that in the middle, where there would usually be sand or a stage, was a temple. Except...it wasn't a temple at all. Greek style columns stood at each corner, and there was a triangular style roof on top of the columns, but the sides were clear glass, turning the whole thing into something reminiscent of a giant fish-tank.

I squinted to make sure I was seeing correctly.

I was.

The thing was filled with water. A large, rocky cave rose up from the bottom of one side of the tank, its entrance angled up into the main body of water. Small, black-and-white fish moved between tall swaying grasses, but the greenery was sparse, and perhaps only for decoration. Kryvo wouldn't like it, I thought as I stared. There was nowhere to hide except the cave. And I got the distinct feeling that was the last place anyone would want to go.

Rows of benches lined the sides of the arena, and the temple-tank was so huge I didn't think there was anywhere you could sit and not get a good view of what was happening inside it. And boy, were there a lot of people looking. The bleachers were filled with spectators. Hundreds and hundreds of Olympian citizens, all cheering and waving banners, had turned out for the spectacle.

I was standing on the top row of the seats, which appeared to have been reserved for the gods, and the competitors.

"Good day Olympus!" roared Atlas' voice. "Please find, in turn, your champions!"

I watched as a bright light shot up from opposite me on the other side of the stadium, like a laser-beam. Kalypso was illuminated, and she waved. The black gown was gone, replaced by tight black leather fighting garb.

Another beam of light went up to her right, illuminating Polybotes. I watched as the light ringed the stadium, lighting up Ceto, Poseidon, then myself.

Poseidon looked as angry as I'd ever seen him, weapons strapped to his chest and hips, and golden armor plating his shoulders. I couldn't help thinking he looked wrong somehow without his trident. The crowd roared for him though, a much bigger cheer than for any of the other competitors. Myself included. I'd barely received a smattering of applause.

"This is a game to win an advantage in the Trials. A warmup, if you will," boomed Atlas' voice. I looked around for him but could see no sign of the Titan. The Olympian gods, minus Zeus, Hera and Aphrodite, were sitting in a box of seats to my left, looking for all the world like they were attending a gladiator show. "Let me tell you more about the first Trial."

A flame the size of a building burst from the triangular tank roof, bright white and fierce. As it died down, an image appeared in the body of the flame. It was a shell. A nautilus shell, the geometric curves just like the one tattooed on my chest.

"The Poseidon Trials will be won by the contestant with the most of these at the end. The first Trial will be a race." The image shifted, and a ship with gleaming golden sails came into view. "To earn both your ship and your starting positions in the race, you will each now face a deadly sea creature. The time it takes to retrieve the ship's flag from the monster's lair is the time you will have to wait before starting the race."

I swallowed.

I couldn't defeat a deadly sea creature.

I had no weapons, no speed, no magic.

"Shit. Shit. Fuck, damn and shit." The cold sweat was back, and I shifted my weight between my feet, scrambling for a plan. "Any ideas, Kryvo?" I hissed.

"Hide?"

I gritted my teeth. Company, he may be, but the little starfish was not going to be useful in a fight.

Atlas's voice rang out again. "First up, Kalypso!"

There was a flash of light, then Kalypso was in the tank. She didn't even have to kick her legs to tread water, her body just hovered in the liquid like it was the most natural thing in the world.

I would have expected her hair to become invisible once she was underwater, given that it was made from water itself. But it didn't vanish at all. Instead, it turned bright violet purple, swishing up and around her face just like real hair.

"She will be facing a giant octopus!"

The water churned opposite her, then shimmered. A giant octopus appeared, with long muscular tentacles that whipped and churned at the water around it. Sticking out of its suckers were wicked dagger-sharp claws and its eyes were pitiless red orbs. I noticed one tentacle had a strange-shaped sucker on the end of it, with a bright red glowing spot, but then the creature attacked, and all my attention moved to Kalypso.

She easily dodged the first swipe, moving through the water like magic, no thrashing or kicking her limbs at all. She swooped and ducked under every lashing of the lethal tentacles, getting beneath the monster and closer to the cave entrance.

In the sand on the tank bottom, directly under the octopus was a glowing green flag, gently waving in the current. As Kalypso reached it the octopus made a screeching sound, flicking the tentacle with the glowing end toward her. She raised her hand, and I saw a short spear in it. Ignoring the green flag, she flicked the spear at the octopus above her. It landed directly in the glowing red spot, and the thing screeched even louder. Kalypso sped up and swam over a second flag just a foot from the entrance to the cave, this one yellow. The octopus moved fast, trying to get back to the entrance of what I was guessing was its lair, before Kalypso reached it.

The movement of the huge creature sent more currents pulsing through the water and I saw a bright blue flag rippling just inside the entrance.

Kalypso was moving so fast that she reached it just before the octopus did, but she didn't swipe up the blue flag. Instead, she kept moving, entering the cave. Dark liquid erupted from the octopus' suckers and one darted into the darkness after her.

I held my breath for a beat, then the octopus screeched a final time, shimmered and disappeared.

Kalypso swam back out of the cave, waving a red flag triumphantly.

"Kalypso reached the most difficult flag in one minute and four seconds," roared Atlas. "The red flag equates to her having a Whirlwind class ship for the race. Congratulations, Kalypso!"

She waved the flag some more, then she flashed white, disappearing from the tank and reappearing in the top row of benches where she'd started.

The crowd cheered loudly as I sat down hard on the bench behind me.

"I'm going to die."

"It is possible," Kryvo said.

Panic was setting in, making my fingertips feel weirdly numb. "What the hell am I going to do?"

"I would suggest not going for the flag that is inside the cave, but for one closer."

"No shit," I muttered. "What's a Whirlwind class ship anyway?"

"I don't know, but I can probably find out."

I rubbed my hand across my face, then back through my hair, pulling on my braid.

I tried to picture myself in the tank with the octopus. What would I have done?

"Next up, Polybotes!"

There was a flash and the giant appeared in the tank.

I stood back up, wringing my hands as I waited to see what the giant would be facing. "He must get past a rotblood!"

The demon shark shimmered into being opposite him. Icy chills rippled over my skin, but the giant had no such fear.

He beat his chest, and it looked as though he was laughing. How was he breathing underwater? I knew Poseidon was the creator of the giants, but I didn't know any of them had water magic.

Polybotes was almost as big as the shark, and it snapped at him, black soulless eyes fixed on his throat. Polybotes raised one massive fist. I frowned in disbelief as the rotblood darted forward and he drew back his arm.

"He's not going to-"

A gasp cut off my sentence as the giant landed a punch square on the end of the rotblood's snout. It spun backward through the water, and the giant kicked his legs, angling down toward the cave. The rotblood was fast though, wheeling and snapping at Polybotes heels. I bit down on my lip as the shark caught one of his massive leather boots. I half expected the giant's leg to come clean off as the shark shook its head from side to side, but Polybotes coiled up, landing punch after punch on the shark's face. Eventually, the thing let go of his boot.

"Remind me to find out what the fuck his footwear is made from," I muttered, as he kicked back down toward the flags.

I was equally surprised when the giant didn't go to the cave, instead swiping up the first green flag. Lifting it high, he gave the shark the finger before it vanished.

"Polybotes gets the Zephyr flag in two minutes and fifteen seconds!" bellowed Atlas' voice.

"Zephyr?"

I felt a little sting on my collarbone, and a vision descended over my own.

"I found something," said Kryvo.

I was about to tell him I needed my sight on the arena, but an image formed before me, and I couldn't help looking.

It was another painting, in gleaming color this time, and it showed four ships with cursive writing beneath.

The largest ship had Whirlwind written beneath it. It was completely clad in metal armoring and had three tall masts. Next to it was a ship labeled as a Typhoon, which looked like a Viking long ship to me. It had two masts and a pointy spike on the front. Next was a Zephyr, which was enormous compared to the others, and had an actual pool in the middle of the deck in the painting. Maybe that was why Polybotes went for the Zephyr, I thought. It was the only ship big enough for him. Lastly was a small ship, wooden and plain. A Crosswind, according to the script below.

"Next up, Ceto!" Atlas' voice reached my ears, and the

vision vanished, the temple-tank and arena coming back into focus.

"Thanks, Kryvo," I whispered.

"And she will be facing an enchelys!"

Poseidon's voice rang out around the arena dome, and I snapped my eyes to him. "Ceto is the mother of enchelys," he boomed. "This hardly seems fair."

"For the purposes of these Trials, Ceto and her brother have waived their powers over the creatures who call them their creators," Atlas replied. "Isn't that right, Ceto?"

The sea-goddess spoke, and it sounded like she was underwater, a gurgling sound to every syllable that instinctively made me think of drowning. "Indeed, Atlas. We wish for nothing but a fair win."

"Commence!"

With a flash, the half sea-monster woman was in the tank.

The water between her and the cave shimmered, and then a snake appeared in the water. And not just any snake. The meanest damn snake I'd ever seen.

It had a mane of spikes around its scaly face, and neon green flashes of color pulsed down its unfeasibly long length. Two probing tentacles jutting out from behind its jaws tested the water, flicking menacingly.

Unlike the last two sea creatures, this thing's bright green eyes seemed to hold a knowing gaze, and I wondered how intelligent it was.

I blinked and almost missed the two lunge for each other. Tail and tentacles swiped and splashed through the liquid, and then they coiled around each other, while the snake's mouth snapped at Ceto's human torso.

Dark red oozed around her, and I didn't know if it was inky liquid like an octopus had, or magic, but the snake's thrashing seemed to slow. She raised her hands high and began to twist, her tentacles still locked in a violent embrace with the snake's tail. She brought her hands together, and the dark red stuff expanded like a firework, filling the tank. The snake spasmed, then went limp, uncoiling itself as it floated down to the bottom of the tank.

Ceto moved through the water like a dart, swiping up the blue flag just inside the cave mouth.

"Ceto wins a Typhoon, in one minutes and forty seconds!"

I sat back down, sucking in air.

I couldn't punch a shark in the face or poison a sea snake. What the fuck was I going to do?

"Next up, your defending ruler, Poseidon!"

The crowd threw up a deafening roar as Poseidon was flashed into the tank. His white hair rose around him as he hovered in the water, muscles bulging under the leather strapping and his face fiercely confident. He held a spear in his right hand in place of his trident, and his left hand was glowing.

I stood up again, leaning forward involuntarily.

"He will be facing a xanosa!"

I shuddered as the creature appeared opposite him. Another monster reserved for kids' nightmares, xanosa were a type of siren. She was almost translucent, gray in color, like a watery wraith. Her bones and organs were visible, glowing red inside her mermaid-like body and wings on her back fluttered in the water as she flicked her tail. Her face was pretty until she slowly opened her mouth. Her jaw seemed to disconnect from the rest of her skull, and a dark, gaping hole appeared in her face. The water before her rippled, and I knew from the stories that she was sending lethal sound through the water toward Poseidon.

But the sea god's left hand rose high above his head, glowed brightly, then exploded with what looked like ropes made from water. They twisted and twirled toward the siren, wrapping her up in seconds, turning her over and over in the tank until she was surrounded by spirals of churning liquid. Poseidon moved through the water faster than any of the others had, and was inside the cave before the siren had stopped spinning.

A heartbeat later he emerged, a red flag in his hand. The siren vanished.

"Poseidon gets a Whirlwind in fifty-six seconds," said Atlas, his gleeful boom distinctly absent.

Bile rose in my throat as I realized I was the only contestant left. I rammed some water-root into my mouth as discreetly as I could, my hands shaking.

"Next up is our wildcard entry," he announced. "Almi, *wife* of Poseidon!" The glee was back in his voice. I barely had time to suck in a breath, before the world flashed white.

CHAPTER 20

*T*he water was warm, and though I had to kick my legs to tread water, I didn't notice any tiredness in my muscles. Poseidon's magic vial was working.

I can do this. I can do this, I chanted in my head, focusing below me, where the flags were. The closest flag. That's all I had to get to, and then I would be flashed back out of the tank.

"Please don't die," I heard Kryvo's terrified voice say.

"Almi will be facing a saraki!"

A what? I'd never even heard of a saraki. Kryvo clearly had though, because he let out a pained squeak.

The water before me shimmered, then revealed a creature I couldn't have dreamed up if I'd tried. Fear made my entire body seize as I tried to take it in.

The size of my shitty old car, it looked like a fish, but half of its whole frigging body was mouth. Hundreds of teeth as tall as me jutted out of its jaws at all angles, and I couldn't avoid seeing down its expansive gullet. It could swallow me whole.

A long arm came out of the top of its head, a glowing orb dangling on the end of it, in front of the monstrous mouth.

I had time to remember something about angler fish luring in prey with a light hanging in front of their mouths, when everything suddenly turned dark.

All I could see was the glowing orb. It seemed kind of far away, and a gentle fog clouded my mind.

Where was I? And why was it dark?

The light would help me. I just needed to reach the light, and I would be able to see what was happening.

I kicked my legs, moving toward the light.

A slight stabbing pain on my collarbone made me pause.

I could hear a distant squeaking, but the pull of the light and the muffled fogginess in my head made it impossible to work out what it was.

I shook my head, trying to clear it, but nothing happened.

The light pulsed, and I refocused on it. It was so pretty. A warm orange glow that promised safety.

I gave another kick of my legs. I needed to reach the light.

Stop.

A male voice boomed through the fog in my head. *Swim down. Now.*

I recognized the voice. Who's was it? My memory wasn't working properly. Nothing was working properly, I realized, a tiny trickle of alarm creeping into my calm.

Swim down. Now. Look for a yellow flag.

But… But the light. I needed to get to the light.

The yellow flag! Now!

Almost against my will, I changed my angle, tipping my head downward through the water. Some of the darkness receded as the orb left my line of sight. A faint glow of green was beneath me, and a little further on, yellow.

Good. The yellow flag. Don't look at the light.

Water churned around me, and more of the serenity that had overcome me leaked away.

Fear replaced it. As the green flag came into reach, the haze lifted completely, and awareness of my situation rushed me.

Christ on a fucking cracker, I'd nearly swum straight into the thing's mouth.

Instinctively, stupidly, I glanced up at the mammoth fish I was swimming under. As soon as the light came into focus, everything around me dimmed again.

Almi!

Wrenching my gaze away, I kicked my legs hard. I reached for the green flag.

The yellow flag. You will not be able to sail a Zephyr, the voice barked.

Poseidon?

It was Poseidon's voice, I realized now that the brain-fog had faded.

Hesitantly, I pulled my hand back from the green flag.

He was helping me. I would be fish-food if he hadn't spoken to me. I had no reason not to trust him.

I kicked my legs hard, heading for the yellow flag instead. The water around me churned suddenly, throwing me off course. I rolled in the water, the fish above me coming into view.

Apparently, it had given up trying to lure me in gently.

I swallowed back a scream as its disproportionately small fins whirred and it powered through the water toward me, its terrifying jaws snapping violently. The light swung before it, and everything around me dimmed and sharpened as my eyes betrayed my instructions and tried to follow it.

I used my arms to pull myself through the water, as low to the sand and out of the thing's reach as I could get.

The yellow flag was only a couple of feet away and I spurred myself forward as my chest hit the sandy bottom.

I lunged for the flag, and as I closed my fingers around it, pain screamed through my ankle. My lips parted as I saw stars, water rushing into my mouth and down my throat.

"Almi gets a Crosswind in four minutes and forty-seconds," I vaguely heard Atlas say, and then I was on the bleachers, gasping for air and choking on water as I crumpled to the floor.

I heaved, water clearing from my airways, my eyes streaming. The pain in my ankle was so intense I thought I might pass out.

"It bit you, oh gods, it bit you," Kryvo was squeaking repeatedly.

I wiped at my eyes and rolled over onto my side, before looking down at my ankle.

If I hadn't just spewed up a load of water, I probably would have thrown up. Blood poured from a gash low on my calf, the skin ragged from the thing's serrated tooth. I was pretty sure I could see bone, and my head swam. I looked away, leaning my head back on the bench and closing my eyes. A deep fatigue washed through me, the pain dulling. Somewhere in my head, I knew that was a very bad thing. But I couldn't fight the darkness pulling me down.

I heard footsteps, then a female voice.

"Fuck, that's nasty. Good job it only grazed you. Let me sort this out."

I forced open my eyes with an effort, and saw the white haired figure of Persephone sitting on the bench above me.

Vines flowed from her palms toward my legs. I was too out of it to respond, and when they wrapped around my thigh a pleasant warmth pulsed out from them. The darkness began to lift.

Then the pain came back full force, and I let out a hissing breath.

"It'll stop hurting in a minute," Persephone said apologetically. After a second, the pain faded, and I felt my shoulders sag in relief.

Atlas' voice echoed around the arena, making them tense again. "That's it for today! Tomorrow we will witness the first Trial of three, to decide who will win Poseidon's trident, and his realm."

"You can look now," Persephone said.

I did, screwing my face up in dread.

The gash was gone. A wide white scar was in its place, and the pool of blood still spread across the sandy ground, but the wound itself was no more.

"Woah." I scrambled into a sitting position and realized that my fatigue had disappeared too. "How did you do that?"

"I'm a goddess of life. I'm good at healing," she smiled at me, the vines unwrapping from my thigh and whooshing back into her palms. "Here. Let me help you up." She held out her hand to me and I took it, steadying myself on her as I stood up. Gingerly, I tested my ankle. It was a bit sore, like I'd twisted it or something, but that was all.

"I can't thank you enough," I said. "Why did you help me?"

"I had my own Trials, and I nearly died a bunch of times," she said, a rueful look on her face. "I won't be able to help you during the actual Trials as that's not allowed, but I'll do what I can otherwise."

Gratitude welled up through me, emotion making my eyes hot. Nobody had looked out for me since I lost Lily. "Thank you," I said, trying to project my sincerity.

"It's nothing," she said. "And well done. You made it through the first test."

"Shit, you're right." A smile sprang top my lips. "I survived!"

She laughed. "Yup. What magic do you have? I'd have guessed water, but the saraki has psychic magic and you resisted it. That's not easy."

She cocked her head at me and I swallowed. I could hardly tell her that I had no magic at all, and that I'd resisted the evil damned thing because Poseidon had helped me.

Why? Why had he helped me?

I looked over at where he had been standing, but there

was nobody there. In fact, the entire arena had almost emptied.

I looked back at Persephone, and an idea slammed into me. "Can you heal anything?"

She shook her head. "No. I'm pretty new to my powers, and I've only recently learned to do that with wounds. I'm pretty good at poisons now, but that's all so far."

I bit down on my lip. "Do you... Do you think you could take a look at my sister?"

Hope was rising inside me. A goddess healer. What wouldn't I have given to have access to a goddess healer before now?

"Is she sick?"

I opened my mouth to answer, but Poseidon's voice sounded behind me. "She is in a sleep induced by powerful magic. You will not be able to help her."

I whirled and saw Poseidon a few rows down on the benches. "You don't know that she can't help," I protested.

"I *do* know that she can't help."

His eyes were hard, his stance resolute.

Persephone touched my arm, drawing my attention back to her. "I must go. If you need me, use this." She passed me a tiny gold rose.

"Thank you," I said, and she vanished with a flash of light.

I turned back to Poseidon, but he spoke before I could. "Persephone can not know of the stone blight," he said.

"Why not? What if she can heal it?"

"She can't."

"You can't possibly know that without her trying."

Anger flashed on his face. "You forget who I am," he snarled. "I know a great deal."

"Then it's about fucking time you shared some of it!" I hadn't wanted to yell at him. I'd wanted to thank him, for saving my life a second time. But here he was, being an absolute prick again. "You can start with what powerful magic put Lily to sleep and why this stone thing has to be a secret."

I put my hands on my hips, then stumbled as he flashed himself to a foot in front of me.

I went from looking down at him on the lower bench, to having to tilt my head back to look up into his eyes.

His huge frame was dripping with water still, and he smelled like... *freedom*. The word popped into my head unbidden, and I didn't understand it. This man represented the opposite of my freedom, in every damned way.

His eyes were stormy with that wild look, and this close, I was sure I could see real waves crashing in them, sparks of silver ocean froth rolling across his irises.

"You test me," he growled. His voice even sounded like crashing waves this close.

"Just tell me. Tell me what you know about Lily." As I stared up at him, the memory of his stern, solid voice pulling me away from the saraki's light came back to me. "Please," I added softly.

His chest tensed, and his hard jaw ticked. "Not here."
"What?"

"I will tell you what you want to know. But not here."
"You will?"

"Yes." To my surprise, he held out his hand. I eyed it suspiciously and he bared his teeth at me. "If you want me to tell you secrets, then we need to be somewhere where they will not be overheard," he said through gritted teeth. "I can't flash you there without contact."

Frowning, I placed my hand in his. Electricity bolted up my arm, exploding in my chest and I gasped. It wasn't painful, it was... delicious. It was fast and powerful and fierce and free and-

"Are you ready?" Poseidon's voice was gruff, and I scanned his face for any hint that he'd felt whatever I just had, but he just wore his normal pissed expression. Wild, or pissed. Those were the only two looks I ever saw on his face. He was a furious force living on the edge of control.

"Yes. I'm ready," I said.

Narrowing his eyes at me, he grunted, then everything went white.

CHAPTER 21

The first thing I was aware of when the light cleared was wind. Cool ocean air whipped across my face, blowing my hair free from its scarf.

"Where are we?" I breathed, turning in a slow circle. It was a space similar to Poseidon's throne room - in that it was round and had columns holding up the ceiling. But the view... We were outside. Not underwater in a golden dome, but above the surface of the ocean.

I stepped toward the edge to peer out. The ocean lapped at the sides of the tower, and birds called in the distance. All I could see for miles was the blue sea against a sky painted in pastel-colored clouds. Another gust of salty ocean air blew between the columns and I breathed in deeply.

"This is my private stables."

"Stables?" I turned to him in surprise, then scanned the space. I saw no animals, just the open area we were standing in, and nothing but a small spiral staircase leading into the plain ceiling.

"You wanted to know about the blight." His expression was tight and controlled. "And the sleep cast over your sister."

I instantly stopped wondering about the stables and stepped back toward the sea god. "Yes."

"The blight has been afflicting all of Aquarius. For some time. I have been keeping it from the citizens."

"Why?"

"I hoped to put an end to it before fear caused problems. I do not believe my people would behave favorably if they thought they might turn to stone."

"They deserve to know! What if they could help stop it?"

He ground his teeth. "I have tried many things to put an end to it. Things far more powerful than Persephone's healing magic. None have worked. And none will."

"How do you know? You can't just give up hope."

"I know because the Oracle of Delphi told me."

I scowled, hatred oozing through me. "Fucking Oracle."

Poseidon flinched. "Do not blame her."

"Why the hell not? She told you to marry me. Is she responsible for Lily's sickness?"

Poseidon faltered before answering. "No. But I am starting to suspect that she is somehow connected to everything that is happening." His gaze sharpened. "And that you are connected too."

I fisted my hands. "I'm just a revenge ticket for a god you pissed off," I snapped. "What does the blight do? You're living with it."

Even as I gestured at him, the stone crept across his

skin, down one pec. I dragged my eyes up from his chest awkwardly.

"I was able to visit a healer powerful enough to keep it at bay, but their magic will wear off."

I raised my eyebrows. "And then?"

"And then it will not matter who wins these Trials to me. I will be as sentient as a statue."

"Shit."

He eyed me. "I concur."

"What did that jerk Oracle say when you saw her?"

His eyes moved from mine to look out over the ocean. "The heart of the ocean is the only thing that can save me and end the blight."

My stomach knotted itself up. So that's why he thought Lily and I were connected to the stone blight. "What *is* the heart of the ocean?" When he didn't reply, I coughed. "If it's a big sapphire and some little old lady threw it in the sea, it's got nothing to do with me."

He turned to me blinking. "What?"

"Guess you've not seen Titanic," I shrugged.

"You are..." He trailed off, and a flash of that wildness shone in his eyes, but it wasn't angry this time.

"Odd?" I offered. "That's what Galatea thinks. But she also thinks I'm plotting to bring you down so..."

"Are you?"

"I just want to cure Lily. That's it." *And steal your ship to do so.*

He cocked his head at me, his hair failing along his jaw. I was nearly overcome with the urge to brush it away and forced myself to step backward.

"Why did you help me today?"

"You would have died if I hadn't."

"You really care about my life, huh?"

His expression tightened. "We've been over this."

But I knew that being married to me hadn't given him his mythical heart of the ocean. So why hadn't he given up on me and tried to find a way to wake Lily up and marry her?

"Right," was all I said. "Well, based on today, I'll be lucky if I survive the next twenty-four hours. Any tips?"

I kept my voice casual, but the reality was that my confidence in surviving the race was zero.

I had no magic, no strength, no speed. I was running on empty, with nothing to back me up. If it weren't for Poseidon I would have swum straight into that freaking fish's jaws, and never even known what happened.

I had to take Kryvo's advice. I had to get the fuck out of the palace as soon as I could. If I couldn't find the ship before the first Trial, I would have to find another way to get to Atlantis.

"Have you sailed a ship before?"

I snapped my eyes to Poseidon's. "No. I spent my childhood underwater." My pulse raced a little as I added, "and ships fly through the sky. They don't work underwater." *Except yours.*

"No. They work via solar sails. The sails on the vessels absorb light, and that powers the ship's magic. They are steered and controlled by thought. The tighter your bond with the ship, the better your control."

"Do any ships work underwater?" I asked.

He frowned. "No. Not unless I make them. You won a Crosswind, and they are the smallest class of ship. It should be easier for you to manage." His face creased into a scowl as he studied my face. "You are planning to leave," he said slowly. There was certainty in his eyes as he moved closer to me.

How could he possibly have known that? "I…" I raised my hands. Was there any point lying to him? "I'm considering it," I said eventually.

"You will not get far."

"Is that a threat?"

He barked a humorless laugh. "If only. Atlas is a powerful, ancient Titan, and these are public Trials. Whether or not either of us like it, this race, and the following two Trials, are happening."

Shit.

"You're sure?"

His expression was grim as he lifted an arm, pushing his hair back out of his face. It seemed such a human gesture, rather than a godly one, and I found myself just a little less intimidated by him. "I am sure." His outrageously blue eyes left mine again, roaming over the ocean. "Atlas will stop at nothing to ensure your death."

A shudder rippled through me. "What did you do to his wife?"

I knew he wouldn't answer me, but I had to try.

"That is my business."

"Would it change things if Atlas knew you didn't care for me?"

When his eyes snapped back to mine, the wildness flared unmistakably, and power pulsed out from him, raw and barely controlled. For a second, I wanted to leap from the edge of the stables and immerse myself the sea, live forever in its unbridled, limitless world of sheer power. In the freedom the ocean offered. *And I wanted to do it with him.*

I blinked at him, and the feeling dissipated. I'd never, ever felt a connection to water like that. And... *And I'd never wanted a man like that.*

"You are weak."

"What?"

"You are weak," Poseidon repeated, matter-of-factly. "Physically," he added, as though that would help soften the insult. It didn't.

"Yeah. I guess. I haven't adjusted well." I shifted my weight.

"You should eat more."

I couldn't help laughing. "I would freaking *love* to eat more. Give me food, oh mighty king, and I will obey your terrible order." I gave him a mocking bow, then jumped in surprise when I straightened. He was inches from me, muscular frame looming over me.

"Do you know how many people mock me?"

I opened my mouth to say something smart, then closed it again. I shook my head, my heart beating hard against my ribs. A powerful gust of wind blew over us, and a whisper of that sense of freedom engulfed me.

"Very few who live afterward," he growled.

"You keep saving my life," I whispered. "Be a shame to kill me over a little light banter."

For a split second I could have sworn I saw amusement spark in his eyes. Then the waves crashed across his irises, the wild look returning. Wild and fierce like the ocean itself. He stepped back, and dammit, I almost reached my hand out to grab the straps of his armor and pull him back.

What the hell was wrong with me? *He's a god,* I told myself. He's supposed to have that effect on people.

"I have something for you." His sentence was clipped, and unexpected.

"Really?"

"To help keep you alive."

"So you're not going to kill me?"

His gaze bore into mine and I squirmed.

"Not today."

CHAPTER 22

I followed Poseidon up the stairs, my heart beating a little too fast in my chest.

We emerged in a round space identical to the one below, except it was ringed with huge half-height stable doors between inset columns. Excitement made my steps quicken as I left the last step of the stairs.

"Is this where the animals are kept?"

"The pegasi. Yes."

I looked toward the nearest stall, hoping to get a glimpse one, but the bottom half of the door was too tall.

"I've never seen one," I breathed.

"You did not attend the academy, where you might have learned to ride one." He didn't word it has a question, and a zing of fear made my chest tighten.

"How do you know that?"

He ignored me, striding to one door and pulling it open, revealing the stall beyond. There was no animal in it, but I could see that the other side was completely open to the air, so the pegasus could come and go as it pleased.

A large amount of hay covered the floor, and ornate-looking iron troughs held both food and water.

"They cannot live in underwater domes as they need to be able to fly at will, so the tower extends high enough to break the surface of the ocean."

I nodded. "I read about them."

Poseidon took a deep breath. "For the duration of the Trials, you may borrow a palace pegasus." A small squeak escaped my lips. "These animals are my personal creations, and unlike most pegasi they can move under the water, as well as through the sky. I believe they will be able to help you both with flying ships and any tests beneath the surface."

I felt my mouth dropping open. "You... You'd really let me have a pegasus?"

"For the duration of the Trials only," he repeated, a strain in his voice. "And these animals are truly special. They have a will of their own. Without my trident, I can't force them to do anything. If they do not like you, they will do nothing to help you."

I nodded my head fervently. "Okay. How do I find one that likes me?"

"You must sense it. Close your eyes, reach out with your power, and go to the stall you are drawn to."

Oh shit. Use my power? Well, I was fucked.

Swallowing, I closed my eyes. *Lily? Kryvo? Any ideas?* I sent the thought out into the ether. Lily's image popped into my head.

Just use your normal senses. You love animals. Feel for the pegasi and pick a stall.

The little starfish remained silent.

A strong current of ocean air blew through the open stable door, and I inhaled deeply, trying to ground myself.

Pick a door, any door.

A tiny sound caught my attention. A whinny? I turned, eyes still closed. There it was again, followed by a distant huffing noise. I moved toward it. If I couldn't use magic, my ears would have to do.

I opened my eyes and found myself in front of three doors. Each had a symbol painted on the wood, but I recognized none of them. I strained to hear anything that would indicate which door had a pegasus behind it. The slight clopping of hooves reached me, and I reached out, moving quickly.

"This one," I said, laying my hand on the wood. A loud whinny went up from the other side, and I snatched my hand back.

To my astonishment, Poseidon smiled. And hell, *was it a smile.* His whole face changed, the constantly angry or out-of-control energy replaced with that of a man who had no worries in the world. He looked like the carefree, sun-kissed surfer every girl would give anything to spend Saturday night with, eyes alive with the promise of endless fun.

I stared at him and his smile faded, as though he'd realized what he'd done but was reluctant to retract it. "That is *galázies apochróseis tou okeanoú.* My wildest animal."

"Oh. That's quite a wild name."

"It means *blue shades of the ocean.*"

He strode over and pulled up the latch. A slight panic

took me. "Wait! Do I need to know anything? How do you talk to a pegasus?"

Poseidon just eased open the door and stood back.

Two eyes, shining like cobalt stars, fixed on mine, and my breath caught.

I'd never seen anything so magnificent as the creature moving slowly out of the stall toward me.

He was the size of a large horse and although his coat was chalky white, his mane and tail were just like Poseidon's eyes. Silver froth and an ombre of ocean blues were running through the hair, making it look as though it was covered in waves as the pegasus moved.

With a loud whinny, the creature snapped its wings out taut, and I gasped in delight. Light rippled across them, a sheen of gold swooshing over every feather as though a layer of liquid metal coated them. He raised his head, nostrils flaring as I stood before him.

"Hi," I said nervously, as I heard Kryvo give a barely audible squeak. *Please don't eat starfish,* I thought as I took a tentative step toward the Pegasus. I was aware of Poseidon's eyes on me as I slowly reached out a hand to the creature. His head was a foot above mine, so I lifted my arm high.

He snorted, making me jump, then stamped his feet. I stood my ground and tried to keep my hand steady.

"I don't have anything to give you, like an apple or... whatever pegasi eat," I said. "But I can tell you that you are the most gorgeous thing I've ever laid eyes on."

The pegasus paused in his stamping and turned his head a little so that he could fix one eye on me.

Hoping it could understand me and was susceptible to

flattery, I continued. "Your wings are just beyond beautiful. And Poseidon here tells me that you can fly through water as well as the sky? That is epic."

The pegasus rustled his wings in what I hoped was appreciation of my words.

"I'm, erm…" I glanced at Poseidon, but his face gave away nothing. "Weak, apparently. And I need a little help with some situations that, well, will probably kill me." I lifted my hands in a what-can-you-do kind of way, and the creature's nostrils flared again. Then he dipped his head and moved a couple of steps closer. My pulse quickened.

"I was kind of hoping, if you've nothing else planned, that you might help me out for a few days?"

The pegasus froze, then snorted, shaking its head.

"Obviously, I wouldn't want to put you in any danger," I said quickly. He lifted his snout and turned to Poseidon. I watched as the god stared into the creature's shining eyes for a long moment.

Eventually, he spoke. "I am sorry, my friend. I can't communicate with you."

There was so much sadness in Poseidon's voice, and the pegasus gave an equally sad whinny. Compassion for the god's loss surged through me, unbidden.

You don't like him, remember! I chided myself silently. *He's made your life hell! Who cares if he can't talk to his animal friends anymore?*

But as Poseidon dropped his head respectfully at the Pegasus, and the creature did the same, I knew I did care. I could feel his connection to the amazing creature, and his sorrow was tangible.

He may treat Nereids like crap, but the man clearly looked after his animals.

With another stamp, the pegasus turned back to me.

"Oh. Hello again," I said, giving a lame little wave. I suppressed a yelp as the thing moved faster than I expected and bumped his cold nose against my hand.

An impression of rushing wind, tangy, cool, ocean spray and roaring waves filled my mind, and laughter bubbled out of my mouth unbidden.

"Blue," I said, the word ringing out in my head.

"He has told you his chosen name. He has accepted you." Poseidon's voice remained soft, but I didn't turn to him.

Blue had backed up, raising and dropping his beautiful wings in some sort of show, and my delighted attention was riveted on him.

"Blue, huh? That's a lot easier to say than your real name." He pranced up and down, flicking his tail and neighing, and I clapped my hands. "You're amazing!"

"Wait until you see the ocean from his point of view."

This time I did turn to Poseidon, the wistful tone of his voice almost painful to hear. I frowned at him. "Why do you say that like you can't?"

"My duties keep me in the palace. Containing this blight and the people it is affecting is a time-consuming job."

"You're the king—surely you can get out for the odd pegasus ride?"

"I do not want to risk passing the blight on," he said, after a long pause.

I stilled, as did Blue. "Is that how it is contracted?"

"We don't know. There is no evidence that it is passed on through physical contact, but I can't risk the life or health of these creatures."

More unwelcome respect for him crept into me. "My friend who has been taking care of Lily has not got it. And I am sure he has been in some contact with her." The thought of her alone in the Silos' bakery made some of the softer feelings I appeared to be having toward Poseidon recede a little.

He nodded. "Those in the city who have fallen ill do not seem to have any link to one another."

"What have you done with them?"

His expression turned sour, and angry. "They are in the palace."

"And their families?"

"We have had to use magic," he said.

I cocked my head at him, unease washing over me. "What do you mean?"

"Until we know how to cure the sick, the families of those afflicted must be kept unaware."

"Define 'unaware.'" I heard my own tone turn sour.

"I had a choice," the god snapped. "Isolate those who know about the blight or remove it from their memory. I took what I believe is the fairest option. I removed their memories."

"Of the blight?"

"Of the person afflicted."

Horror coursed through me. "You made people forget about their loved ones?"

"Only temporarily. Even gods can't remove memories permanently, not without drinking from the river Styx."

His tone was granite now, and I knew he would not tolerate my insolence much longer, but I couldn't help my outrage.

"You have no right to do that!" I'd lived with the memory of my sister as my only companion for so long that the thought of not even knowing she existed made me feel sick.

"It is temporary," he growled. "They feel no sadness, and their lives are not impacted in any way."

"Just because they don't know it, doesn't mean they are not impacted!"

"You would prefer I told them their loved ones were dead?" he roared, making me flinch with the sudden loss of temper. "To tell them they are nothing but lifeless statues that I failed to save!"

Blue whinnied and backed into the stall as Poseidon advanced on me. His words rang through my head. *Failed to save.* He was angry that he had failed to save his people.

"Why do you have to keep the blight a secret? Why not just tell the citizens and make them aware you are trying to fix it?"

"Because." He snarled, coming to stop a foot from me and towering over my smaller frame. "If the world knew I couldn't heal it I would be challenged. It is not possible to show weakness when you are the king of the ocean, and Zeus' brother." His voice was venom, and it took all my courage to stand my ground. The whole tower rumbled with distant thunder and rain had begun to lash down into the sea beyond, making it churn. I took a shaking breath as he continued. "I thought my brother would challenge me if he discovered I, or my realm, was sick. I didn't not expect Atlas." Emotion was sparking in his eyes. Emotion that wasn't anger, it was something deeper, something intense, something raw. "You were not supposed to be a part of this."

My own emotions were reflecting his, growing inside me, fueled by his fierceness. "Why do you care?" I could see in his eyes and hear in his words, that he did.

And I didn't understand.

The fury of the building storm coursed through me. "Marrying me hasn't given you your stupid heart of the ocean. I'm nothing to you!"

Thunder cracked and the wind whipped up, beating at us where we stood, face to face and inexplicably furious.

"You!" Poseidon shouted, then tore his eyes from mine, flinging an arm out. Waves surged up behind him, so high they blocked out the sky.

"I what? For the love of the gods, what?"

He raised another hand, and a tidal wave the size of a skyscraper crashed down over the stables. I sucked in a breath, my whole body tense, ready to be washed away. But not a drop of water entered the stables.

"You make me fucking crazy!" Poseidon bellowed, then with a flash of white light, he was gone.

My limbs were shaking as I stared at the spot he had vanished from. The ocean still churned around me, rain pelting down to be instantly absorbed by the endless sea.

"Is this what happens when the king of the ocean throws a temper tantrum?" I muttered, staring out at the storm and trying to calm my racing heart.

A quiet snicker answered me, and I turned slowly to Blue's stall. Hoof by cautious hoof, he moved toward me.

"You've seen him lose his shit before?" I asked the pegasus gently. Blue shook his stunning mane. "I'm gonna take that as a yes." I stepped closer and felt a tiny sting on my collarbone.

"Shit, Kryvo, I'm sorry," I said, lifting my hand to my shoulder. I'd totally forgotten about him. "You okay?"

"No." The little starfish's voice was as wobbly as I felt. "No, I am not okay. I don't know what's worse, that saraki or Poseidon."

"Yeah," I said, but I didn't mean it. I stared out over the tumultuous sea as the starfish suckered his way slowly onto my palm. Whatever the hell had just happened had irrevocably shifted my opinion of the sea god.

He cared about his people. He was doing the wrong thing, for sure, but not for the wrong reasons. He cared for his animals too, and I didn't think he mourned the loss of his trident for the power it had cost him, but for the removal of his ability to talk to the creatures of his realm.

And... I was truly starting to believe that he cared for me. His smile sang in my mind, an image, so utterly at odds with his normal persona, but so perfectly right somehow.

"He can't care for me," I said aloud, as Kryvo settled in my palm, bright red again.

"Poseidon?"

"Yeah. He doesn't even know me. How could he possibly care for me?"

"He sure gets mad with you for someone who doesn't know you," he said, giving a little shudder.

Blue whinnied, and I looked up at him. "Do you eat starfish?" I asked him. The pegasus stamped his feet, ducking his head low. "Hmmm. I think that's a no. But just in case, please don't eat this one. He's my only friend."

Kryvo heated in my hand as I moved closer to the Pegasus. "I'm your friend?"

"You just faced a lethal sea monster with me. Of course you're my friend."

"I didn't do anything. I tried, though. I was telling you to stay away from the light, but I was too quiet." He sounded so dejected that my heart warmed with sympathy for him. I knew what it was like to feel useless.

"We survived. And I appreciate you trying, so much."

"This is true. We did survive." He sounded a touch more cheerful.

"And now, we have a new friend. This is Blue."

I held him up to the Pegasus, who flared his nostrils and snorted. "He smells," Kryvo announced.

Blue stamped his hooves, and I pulled Kryvo back into my chest. "Maybe don't insult him," I whispered to the starfish, before telling Blue loudly, "You smell amazing." I reached out my empty hand, hoping he would nudge it again. After a small hesitation, he did.

"Blue usually hates everyone." I whirled at Galatea's voice.

"Huh. We're a good match then," I snapped back at her. I wasn't in the mood for her shit.

"You did well today."

"What?"

"Honestly, I didn't think you'd survive. So far, I've seen no evidence that you even have any power. If it weren't for Poseidon's insistence that you do-"

"Why are you here?" I interrupted her. I glanced down

169

at my palm to see that Kryvo had camouflaged himself perfectly, but I didn't know how long she'd been watching me.

"Poseidon sent me to take you back. Unless you'd like to try yourself?"

I considered her words, it only taking me a second to realize that I was totally trapped on the platform out on the ocean.

"Fine." I turned back to Blue. "If you could help me out tomorrow, I'd be super grateful." He locked his shining, intelligent eyes on mine and snorted. "Thanks," I beamed at him, and prayed to anyone who was listening that the beautiful flying horse would show up if I needed him.

CHAPTER 23

*T*here was a frigging feast waiting for me when Galatea deposited me back in my room. "Is this all for me?" I gaped at her.

"Yes. And Poseidon has decided that you don't need to be locked in." She looked as though she thought that was a terrible idea, but I knew why. He'd made it crystal clear that there was no point in running. "The Trial is at dawn tomorrow, so you can spend the rest of this evening in the palace as you wish."

A childish excitement whipped up inside me at the thought of exploring the epic building. *And maybe finding the ship.* "Okay. Thanks."

With one last suspicious look, she left me alone with my ridiculously large, but well earned, feast.

When my stomach was full of pastry and beef, followed by liberal helpings of chocolate, I strapped my belt back on and headed out to explore the palace. And hopefully get an idea of where Poseidon kept his ship.

Just thinking about the sea god made my head spin, and an annoying mixture of emotions churn up in my stomach.

"Kryvo," I said firmly, trying not to think about Poseidon and focus on the task at hand. "Any of your statue friends know where one might keep a ship in this palace?"

The starfish was back on my collarbone. His tiny squeak reached me. "No. I can see some nice gardens though."

"Okay. How do I get there?"

I walked down the corridor until I reached a grand staircase lined with statues. It curved gently downward, and more gold paintings delicately adorned the walls. As I descended I noticed little stone starfish on lots of the statues, whether they were busts of people or depictions of sea creatures.

"Are these what you can see through?" I asked Kryvo, reaching out and touching one that was riding on the back of a leaping dolphin.

"Yes."

I carried on down the staircase until it leveled out in an enormous round hall. There were bridge-corridors leading off it on all sides and I guessed I must have been in a pretty central tower. In the center of the atrium was a fountain, a likeness of Poseidon holding his trident high standing twenty feet tall, as water leaped and played around his legs in a kind of dance.

I walked up to it, frowning. "Bit full of himself," I muttered. "How do I get outside?"

"There's another staircase, along the corridor with the manta ray statue," answered Kryvo. I followed his instructions, finding a staircase leading down at the end of a short bridge-corridor. At the bottom was a set of doors, and when I pushed through them, I found myself at the start of a path with tall green hedges on either side of me. I looked up, seeing the towering white spires of the palace all around me, and the gold of the dome ceiling shining against the blue ocean overhead.

I made my way down the path, which curved gently left and right, the high hedges blocking my view of anything on ground level until I reached an archway.

"Wow," I breathed, as I stepped through. Garden was too polite a word for the space. It was stunning. I was standing at the top of a tiered area, leading down to a massive pool. Rather than meet the edge of the dome to willow people out, this pool appeared to be for actually swimming in. Surrounded by golden tiles, the water was an unnaturally bright blue.

Arches made of twisted wood and draped in purple flowers framed steps that weaved down through the tiers. Flower beds displayed almost exclusively purple and yellow flowers, many of them creepers that wound their way around benches and statues of water creatures.

Green turf covered the ground everywhere, and the color was somehow energizing when I was getting so used to seeing the blue backdrop of the ocean.

I strolled along the paths, trying to work out what I could do next.

I drew on Lily's image, and she materialized in my mind. "I don't know where to look for the ship," I told her.

If the ship is as special as the book says it is, then he is likely to keep it hidden.

"But this is his palace, why would he need to hide it here?"

Hundreds of people live and work here. Including Silos' dad, she reminded me.

"Hmmm."

Have you considered telling him what you know about Atlantis? He may willingly take you.

"The thought had occurred to me." Poseidon believed I had something to do with all this, and he'd said we would 'fix it' after the Trials. Asking him about the healing font may be a lot easier than trying to find it on my own. "If it was likely to work, then he would have tried already," I said. "He said he'd tried lots of powerful things to cure the blight."

There must be a reason he hasn't.

"Or he has, and it didn't work," I said glumly. "Or maybe the book is fiction, and Atlantis doesn't exist." I kicked at a stray tuft of grass creeping up between the slabs under my feet. "Making all of this for nothing."

Dear sister, I believe you would have ended up here eventually, regardless.

"Why?"

Atlas. He wants revenge. He would have found you, just to hurt Poseidon. Revenge is a most powerful motive.

I scowled. "I wonder what Poseidon did to his wife? Killed her? Slept with her? Left her in the human world for years by herself?"

It doesn't matter now. What matters is surviving these Trials. Then, you can work together to find a cure and save Aquarius.

"Save Aquarius? I'm saving you, not the whole damn realm."

I rather think that they're one and the same goal now.

"Shit." I hadn't thought about it like that. But she was right. I groaned. "You know Lily, the fates really fucked this up. It should be you doing all this. I bet you could defeat a demon angler fish, and fly a ship, and breathe underwater, and-"

Enough, Almi. You have what you need to get through this. And now you have a cowardly but smart starfish and a slightly scary pegasus to help you. Her mental image smiled at me, and a tiny bit of confidence snuck through the swamp of self-doubt.

"This is true."

"Who are you speaking to?" The deep voice startled me, and I whirled as I recognized it.

"Atlas."

He was standing beside a statue of a naked mermaid, her arms raised above her head and her eyes closed.

"Almi. Wife of Poseidon." He took a step closer to me, and my pulse quickened. He was wearing robes, formal and black and clasped with his sigil. His skin was so pale he looked like a statue himself, and he oozed a tingling power that felt nothing like the sea.

"Does Poseidon know you are here?"

He spread his hands wide. "We are all here now. Every contestant is residing within this dome." His smile didn't

175

reach his eyes, which were hard. The dark irises were ringed in red, I realized as he moved even closer.

"Why aren't you competing?"

He snorted. "I don't want control of this shitty, water-logged realm."

Defensiveness flashed through me. "Aquarius is too good for you," I spat.

His smile widened, even as his eyes hardened. "Poseidon is responsible for pain you can't even imagine. He will feel it himself, I swear."

"What did he do?" I took a step back as he tried to close the gap between us.

"Ask him yourself." He raised his eyebrows. "Unless you already have and he's refused to tell you?"

I opened my mouth but the truth must have been written on my face.

Atlas laughed. "Good luck tomorrow, little Almi. You're going to need it." A blanket of heat engulfed me, a warning hum of power laced through it, and I felt my knees start to bend.

"You will honor the right gods soon," he hissed, as my kneecaps met marble, and the rest of my body folded into an unwilling bow. "For as long as you are alive, at least." His power was massive, his presence becoming painful, and I screwed my face up as I tried to resist him. His message was crystal clear. He was just as powerful as Poseidon. Possibly even more.

The pressure on my body and the oppressive electric heat vanished, and I raised my head with relief. He gave me one last hatred-filled look, and then he was gone, striding away through the courtyard.

"What the hell was that about?" I whispered.

"I don't like him," squeaked Kryvo.

"That makes two of us."

What had Poseidon done to his wife?

CHAPTER 24

I woke with a start, the heavy book across my chest making me panic.

A knocking sounded at my door, loud and insistent, and I blinked around myself.

I'd fallen asleep reading about flying ships, I realized. Was it dawn already?

"Who is it?"

I expected Galatea to answer, but Poseidon's gruff voice barked, "Open the door."

I shuffled my legs off the bed, my muscles stiff from falling asleep in such an awkward position. Nerves blasted my sleepiness away though as I pulled open the door.

"Why knock? Surely you can just barge your way in?" I scowled at him. He was dressed in his leather fighting garb, and droplets of water glistened on his bare chest. I forced myself to remember that we didn't get on. "It's your palace after all, and you're good at taking what you want without asking."

He bared his teeth at me. "We have an hour before the Trial begins. I came here to show you what to do with the ship, but if you're going to be difficult—"

I held my hands up, cutting him off. "I may be difficult, but I'm not stupid. Give me ten minutes to get ready."

He just grunted and folded his arms. Trying not to notice what that did to his biceps, I slammed the door shut.

As fast as I could, I showered and dressed in identical, but clean clothes from the closet. "Kryvo, I know you're not going to want to come, but you helped me out last time, and honestly? I would appreciate the company." The starfish rippled red on his cushion on the dresser.

"I thought you might say that. Are you absolutely sure we can't hide?"

"One hundred percent, little friend."

He let out a squeaky sigh. "I will do what I can to help us survive. Although I sort of wish I'd never met you."

"Charming." I let him squish his way onto my palm, then lifted him to my shoulder. Strapping on my belt, I looked at my reflection in the mirror.

"Oh Lily. This really should be you," I sighed, my stomach knotting with trepidation.

There was another bang on the door, and I clenched my jaw tight and shook my head.

But it was me. I had to do it, for both of us.

Poseidon gave me a cursory look as I stepped out of my bedroom door, then, with no warning everything flashed white.

"Hey!" I spluttered as the light faded and I stumbled. "You could have told me you were about to do that!"

"Be quiet."

I bristled, but my surroundings caught my attention before I could reply.

We were standing on a pier, and there were real ships in front of me. Real big-ass ships.

We were outside too, above the surface of the ocean, and the breeze was warm as it blew across us.

"Where are we?"

"That is Sagittarius." He pointed behind me and I turned to see that the pier we standing on was attached to an island.

"Artemis' realm? Isn't Sagittarius a forbidden realm?"

"Nowhere is forbidden for one as powerful as me."

I pulled a face. "Right. Of course not, oh mighty one." He growled low in his throat, and I tried to look vaguely meek. "Why are we here?"

"This is where the race will commence. It is the nearest coastline to Aquarius."

"How do you know this is where the race will start?"

"It is where I would start it. And I originally designed these Trials. Although I am sure Atlas will make some alterations."

"Oh."

"This is a Crosswind." He turned back to the pier and pointed at the smallest ship.

The wooden hull loomed over me, and I stared up at it.

Something stirred in my gut, something fluttery and just beyond my reach. Putting it down to fear that this was all getting very real, and I would be about to face a Trial that would likely kill me, I looked at Poseidon.

"I can't see anything except the hull," I said.

Everything flashed white again, but this time, I didn't trip as we materialized on wooden planks.

"Thanks for the heads up," I ground out sarcastically.

To my surprise, he flicked a look at me that was definitely an equally sarcastic 'you're welcome'.

"This is the main mast."

I looked where he was gesturing, and the fluttering in my stomach intensified. The sails were *glorious*.

Glorious.

There was no other word for them. They were like fabric made of metal, gleaming with silvers and golds as they rippled in the wind, the light moving over them almost like liquid flames.

Following my gaze, Poseidon spoke softly. "They absorb and use light. They are quite something to look at."

"They're fucking ace," I breathed.

"I don't know what that means, but I shall take your look of awe as a positive reaction."

I nodded my head in agreement.

"The bridge is here, and that is where the ship's wheel is."

I dragged my eyes from the sails to where he was pointing. But my gaze didn't skim past him as I intended it to. My breath caught, my stomach almost flipping in its jittery ferocity.

He looked as he had most of the previous times I had seen him; leather boots and pants, weapon straps crisscrossing his powerful body, his hair blowing around his hard, fierce face. But on the ship, framed as he was by the rich-colored wood of the planks, the light reflecting from the sails, and the rolling waves of the ocean beyond...

He looked *right*. So damned right, I couldn't take my eyes off him.

"You belong here," I said, without meaning to.

He faltered, emotion flaring in his eyes. "What?" The word was soft, wary even.

"You just... You just look right here. On the deck."

Every hard plane on his body drew me in, the tanned skin of his abs disappearing into his waistband so suddenly, glaringly, deliciously. Images of us together on the ship, the roaring wind and fierce ocean around us nothing compared to the passion in his stormy eyes as his mouth took mine-

"No. I belong in Aquarius, under the sea, with my brethren."

"Then why..." I didn't know how to finish my question. Why did he look so utterly perfect here, out in the open?

Where in the hell were these thoughts coming from?

I felt my face flush, and I dropped my eyes to the planks.

"Ship's wheel," he said, slowly.

"Ship's wheel," I repeated, looking over at the bridge.

"It is easier for most to guide the ship with the wheel. If you are bonded with the ship, you can just touch the wood of the mast. But bonding takes time. Time we don't have."

"Right," I said, though I was barely listening. I was too busy scolding my ridiculous, apparently romance-starved brain.

"To steer, just think where you want to go."

"Sounds easy," I said, forcing a fake cheeriness into my voice.

"It is not easy," he said. "We will, no doubt, have to do more than just steer the ship. You will have to concentrate on both that and whatever Atlas throws at us." He paused. "Why are you not looking at me?"

Because my brain keeps threatening to mentally remove your pants ever since we got on this stupid ship? "I'm just nervous."

"You should be. Come." He strode to the small set of steps leading up to the bridge, and I followed him. When he started to climb, I made sure my eyes were fully averted from his ass in the tight leather, staring out absently at the island of Sagittarius. It mostly looked like scrubland, nothing more than hardy weeds peeking out of the sand on the narrow shore.

"I said come."

"Right." Snapping my eyes back I saw that Poseidon had ascended the steps.

I moved up them quickly and took a second to study the ship properly.

The deck stretched in front of me, the solar sails dominating my view. The masts and sails apparently needed no rigging, as I could see no ropes. The ship narrowed at the front, which I was sure was called the prow, and I saw one single weapon mounted there, possibly a harpoon.

At the back of the raised bridge was a large wooden chair, bolted to the deck, and some sort of contraption on wires - a large box. The whole ship was made of a deep, rich-colored wood, and the railings that wrapped around the entire deck were waist high and quite intricately carved in the shape of waves.

"Touch the wheel."

I lifted my hand to my temple in a salute. "Yes, sir."

I moved to the huge ship's wheel. I couldn't count the spokes, it had so many. When I laid my fingers on it, the wood was warm and welcoming. I closed my fingers around two handle-ended spokes.

"Imagine the ship lifting."

I closed my eyes and did as he told me. I felt a slight lurch, then became aware of a smooth movement under my feet. I opened my eyes, and a grin leaped to my face. We were moving, lifting higher in a vertical motion.

"Good. Now stop."

I willed the ship to stop, and it did. "No way."

Poseidon walked to the rails and looked over. Unable to contain my curiosity about how high I'd taken the ship, I let go of the wheel and joined him.

Peering over the edge, my grin widened. We were a hundred feet over the pier now, and the other ships there looked small. I looked toward the island and saw that the scrubby shore was misleading, as just a few feet further inland was a rich green meadow.

"Can I make it go fast?"

Poseidon looked at me, one eyebrow raised and a hint of *something* in his eyes.

"Yes, I think you probably can. It is unusual for control to come to beginners that easily."

I shrugged nonchalantly, while fireworks of excitement went off in my head. "Maybe it's because I'm a

Nereid," I said, taking the opportunity to reinforce my make-believe powers.

"I doubt it."

I scowled at him. "Why?" I instantly wished I hadn't asked.

He sighed and leaned his elbows on the railings. "I know you have no magic."

Ice cold fear doused me. "What? No."

"That's why I thought you'd have trouble with the ship. I am pleased to see that's not the case. You might actually survive this." He was staring out at the sea, not meeting my flustered face.

"I..." I scrambled for any reason I might not have my magic, any lie I could tell. Lily's voice telling me all my life that I must keep my broken powers a secret rang in my head.

Slowly, Poseidon straightened, turning to me. "I am the king of the ocean. I sense water magic in places you wouldn't even know existed. Did you really think I wouldn't know you were without power?" His voice wasn't hard or angry. It was matter of fact.

"Why didn't you say so before? Why did you let me pretend?"

He stared at me. "It's not important. Your tattoo," he said abruptly, pointing to my chest. My shirt was open over my bandeau vest, the shell clear.

"What about it?"

"Nereid's tattoos are supposed to be vibrant in color."

"Mine's broken." I couldn't keep the bitterness from my voice.

"If I know this, so will Atlas. So will Kalypso. They are

both powerful gods." He glanced at my belt. "Water-root and gadgets will not get you past them."

Embarrassment and shame made my cheeks flame and anger take over my thoughts. "Making me feel stupid and weak isn't going to help me survive," I said through gritted teeth.

"Almi, that is not my intention." Sincerity laced his tone, measured control still governing his expression. "I am trying to prepare you."

"I'm as good as human. How the fuck am I supposed to prepare for this?"

Somehow, not having to keep it a secret anymore made it more real, and tears pricked my eyes as my stomach continued to knot itself.

Poseidon held out his hand, a vial appearing in it. "This will help. And you are a natural with the ship. That might well be enough."

"This is what gave me strength yesterday?" I said, taking the vial from him.

"Yes. It is the best I can do. That and hope Blue comes."

"Why are you helping me?"

"Why do you keep asking me that?"

"I'm broken. You married the wrong Nereid. So why do you care if I live?"

Finally, some of the control slipped from his face. His shoulders tensed as his jaw worked. "Do you want to die?"

"No."

"Then stop questioning me, and just do as you're damned well told." I opened my mouth to respond but he spoke again, "Practice with the ship," he barked, then flashed away.

CHAPTER 25

"*H*e knows, Lily. He's known all the time." I gripped the ship's wheel, staring at the spot Poseidon had vanished.

That's a good thing. I should have known he would be aware.

A gust of wind blew over me as I tried to control my roiling emotions.

Kryvo's squeaky voice carried to me. "You thought he didn't know you were without magic?"

I closed my eyes. "You knew too, huh?"

"Well, yes."

It's one less thing to worry about. Practice with the ship.

I opened my eyes. "Why didn't he tell me?"

I don't think you'll believe me, but I think he didn't want to embarrass you.

"What?"

I can think of no other reason than for him to play along with your lie.

I shook my head, and the scarf keeping my hair back

187

came loose. Wind picked up strands of my hair, the purple color whipping in front of my eyes making me stare.

Of course he knew. I didn't even look like a proper Nereid.

Practice with the ship.

"Can't I have five fucking minutes to feel sorry for myself?" I snapped.

Absolutely not.

"Fine!"

I tied my hair back angrily, then squeezed the wood of the wheel. I willed the ship forward. My anger must have spilled into the command, because we lurched forward so fast I immediately fell over. I landed sideways, my knee taking the brunt of the impact, and I swore loudly.

Concentrate, said Lily.

"Or hide," offered Kryvo.

With a deep breath of clear ocean air, I tried to focus. All this shit with Poseidon would have to wait. Lily was right. I needed to concentrate on surviving the race. And if I did, I could reward myself by yelling at the baffling watery ass all I liked.

I had ten minutes to practice with the ship before Poseidon appeared on the deck beside me.

"It's time," he said, and gave me no chance to respond.

With the next flash of light, we were back on the pier.

Kalypso, Polybotes and Ceto were there too. The scrubby shore was now filled with a crowd of spectators, and to my complete astonishment, I saw Silos among them, standing beside his father. When he caught my eye, he beamed and called out with the rest of the crowd, lifting a banner high.

"Almi to win," it read.

He yelled something that to my average lip-reading skills looked like, "You're doing amazing," and I waved gratefully at him.

There was a resounding boom, and the crowd's cheering fell silent. All the ships at the dock had vanished. With a flurry of glittery swirls, five new ones appeared, hovering a few feet above the surface of the water.

"Kalypso and her Whirlwind!" roared Atlas' voice, and fireworks erupted from the deck of something that looked like it could survive a nuclear holocaust, never mind a race. The hull was clad in gleaming silver armor, and hundreds of cannon tips peeked out of portholes lining both sides. Three masts held gargantuan solar sails, and a harpoon was mounted on the high bridge.

Kalypso waved at the crowd, then a jet of water burst up from under the pier. She stepped gracefully onto it, and it shot upward to deposit her on the deck of the warship.

Acid burned in my chest, nerves making me wring my hands together.

"Poseidon and his Whirlwind!" With a glance at me that was so brief I might have missed it, Poseidon flashed onto the deck of his ship.

"Polybotes and his Zephyr!"

The giant's ship was so big that it appeared to have a bridge at both ends, raised high and sporting wheels as big as cars. The giant stamped along the pier, crouched low, then launched himself up into the air. I would never have guessed a being so large could jump so high. My mouth fell open as he caught hold of a porthole halfway up the hull, then swung himself up to the next one. In seconds, he was pulling himself over the railings. The crowd hooted and cheered as he waved.

"Ceto and her Typhoon!"

The sea goddess immediately dove off the side of the pier. A beat later, I saw her form slithering up the side of the hull of the only ship that looked like a longboat, with a small extra sail and an enormous spike adorning the front.

How the hell was I going to get onto the deck of the last ship; the small, unassuming Crosswind?

I felt dizzy with nerves as Atlas' voice rang out.

"And Almi and her Crosswind!"

I lifted a foot, desperately trying to think of a way onto the ship, when I heard Poseidon's voice in my head.

The box at the back.

I sped up, jogging past the huge hulls of the other ships, their occupants gazing down at me as I passed. When I reached the Crosswind, I saw the crate on wires at the back, only this time it was lowered over the edge of the railings instead of sitting on the bridge. Was it like some sort of elevator?

It's called a hauler. Get in it.

I saw that one of the sides was actually a door and stepped into the box. When nothing happened, I laid my hand on the wood of the box, and willed myself to rise. With an ominous creak, the crate rose.

When it came to a stop, I pushed the door open

nervously. The bridge of the Crosswind came into view, the wheel standing proud in the middle

"Thank fuck for that," I muttered as I hurried to it. I gripped the spokes. "Hi, ship. I'm Almi, and I really, really hope you're going to help me out today."

The wood heated under my hands, and a tendril of confidence snaked through me.

I could do this.

You can do this, Lily agreed.

"It's too late to hide now, right?" said Kryvo.

"Citizens of Olympus!" There was another firework of red light, high in the sky, then Atlas's face formed in the sparks.

"Let me tell you, and the competitors, the rules of the race. You will see rings like this,"—a shining red hoop appeared in the sky next to his face—"along the course. Each one you fly your ship through will reveal more of a map to the finish line. Only once you have flown through all nine rings, will you know where to end the race. You will find the rings in sets of three. The first to cross the finish will receive five shells. The competitor who comes second will get four, the third three, fourth will receive two, and the last will receive one." The image of his handsome face smiled, and his hand appeared, holding a gleaming nautilus shell. Malice sparkled in his eyes. "And trust me when I tell you, you need these shells."

The number of shells didn't matter to me. All I had to do was stay alive.

"If your ship leaves the boundary of the Trial, you will be alerted." His eyes glinted even more wickedly, and I assumed it would be a painful alert. "I'll help you all out to start. The first ring is a mile to the west of Sagittarius. Poseidon, you won the last test, so you start. Three, two, one, go!"

The Whirlwind launched high into the air, and my stomach twisted as I watched him speed away, toward the west of the island. After a moment, Atlas spoke again. "Time's up. Kalypso, you may go!" Her Whirlwind sped after Poseidon's.

Polybotes went next, then Ceto. By the time my four-and-a-half-minute deficit was up, my hands were sweating on the spokes.

"Lastly, Almi!" His image disappeared from the sky as I willed the Crosswind into the air.

CHAPTER 26

*R*elief powered through me as the vessel lifted, the gleaming sails shining bright. As I spurred the ship in the direction the others had gone, an unexpected rush of exhilaration blasted through me. The wind was warm as we soared through the sky, and I could still smell the tang of the ocean below.

Maybe it wasn't Poseidon that had felt right on the ship, I thought as the Crosswind sped through the clouds. Maybe it was me.

The other ships were too far ahead for me to see anything of them, but it wasn't long before I could see something else, gleaming red high above the water.

Giant, flaming hoops.

"Let's do this," I said. Agility was something I might even be better at than some of the others, given the ship's apparent willingness to follow my mental commands.

The ship powered toward the first ring.

A jet of water burst from the ocean below, clipping the side of my ship as we sailed through the air.

I suppressed a shriek of surprise and angled the ship the other way. If I hadn't looked over, I would have missed the second jet, blasting up on my other side. Swearing, I weaved the ship between them, wishing I had more eyes.

"Kryvo! Can you watch my left?"

"Put me on the wheel!"

One handed, I plucked the little starfish from my collarbone, and set him down on the wheel, all while trying to avoid the jets of water. Over half of them were hitting me, taking all the speed out of the ship as it rocked left and right.

"I'm on it! In thirty feet, you got a big one!" His squeaky voice only just carried to me, but it was enough.

With his help, I reduced the hit rate of the jets to well under half, and none of them were square on.

We were fast approaching the first ring when a jet shot up on our right, and I realized something was different about it. It was red.

"What-" I started, then froze in horror.

Crabs. In the jets. Giant, beady-eyed, vicious looking crabs.

"Ooh crap," I hissed, as they began to leap from the jet of water onto the deck of the ship. One landed on the bridge, and began to scuttle toward me. I kicked out at it, the movement making me let go of the wheel. I felt the ship lurch to a stop as my boot connected with the knee-high, bright scarlet crab. The thing went flying backward as I sprang back to the wheel.

"To the hoop!" I urged the ship, as two more crabs ran

at me. The ones on the deck had yet to figure out how to get up the steps, thank the gods.

I kicked away the crabs as they came at me, but I didn't have enough power to get them over the railings, so they just straightened themselves out and came back. Another jet of water burst up on the left, Kryvo yelling something about listening to him and not getting us killed. More crabs flooded onto my ship, and another four of them made it onto the bridge.

Fuck. I couldn't deal with seven *and* control the ship.

I became aware of a change in the light, and glanced up from the claw clacking crabs just in time to see the ship swoop through one of the rings.

"Yes!" I swung my head round, looking for a map.

"The sail!" squeaked Kryvo.

There, on the main sail, a dark ink drawing was appearing. I didn't have time to inspect it though. Pain lanced through my foot, and I looked down to see a crab right in front of me, nipping at my boots. I punted it as hard as I could, and it went flying at another two. Almost like skittles, they collided and skidded across the deck.

"To the next hoop!" I yelled at the ship. I didn't know if commanding it vocally made any difference, but the words came anyway.

I dipped my hand into a pouch on my belt, and pulled out the same little box that had saved my ass in Oxford. With a small prayer, I pressed the button and threw it down on the planks. The hologram elephant sprang to life, the light flickering as it raised its trunk.

All the crabs froze. I watched them just long enough to

ensure they were distracted by the hologram, and then turned back to the sail. Mercifully, the jets had abated.

The corner of a map had appeared on the main mast, the blackness of it stark against the gleaming metallic surface.

I tried to make sense of it, but there wasn't enough to work anything out.

Instead, I focused on the next hoop as the Crosswind powered toward it.

I was ready this time, when a jet shot up as we approached. This one though, was green.

Expecting green crabs to be waiting in the jet of water, I veered hard out of the way. The crabs already on the deck chittered angrily as they slid, and I had an idea.

Kneeling and scooping up the hologram chip, I gripped the wheel hard.

"Hold on, Kryvo," I said, then mentally asked the ship to tilt. It obliged, and the crab chitters turned to tiny clattery shrieks as the deck moved to a ninety-degree angle. I wrapped my arms around the wheel and clung on, grateful for the strength Poseidon's vial had given me. There was no way I could have held on otherwise.

When all the crabs were scrabbling around on the now horizontal railings, I held my breath, clutched the wheel, and willed the ship to tip them over the edge as quickly as possible.

With a jerk, the ship did just that. My feet slipped on the deck and for a terrifying moment I was hanging on with just my arms, but it righted itself fast, leaving me panting as I dropped to my knees.

"Good job," I gasped, stroking the wood. "Clever ship."

Another green jet burst up on my left, and I was so wrapped up in recovering from turning the ship sideways that I didn't have time to react.

I leapt to my feet as animals jumped from the water to my ship.

And they weren't crabs this time.

They were lobsters. Huge green things, with even snappier claws, and tails that curled up over their backs like a scorpions.

"Oh man. Kryvo, you got a good grip there?" I asked him as I kicked out at a fast-approaching lobster-scorpion-thing.

"Yes!" he squeaked.

"Here we go again, then."

By the time we got through the next hoop, I felt sick from all the rolling. The muscles in my arms were beginning to ache every time I held on, but it was working. The ship tipped the vile little creatures off the deck every time I willed her to.

I wasn't sure when I'd decided that the ship was a she, but I was positive she was.

"Last one," I gasped, willing the ship toward the last gleaming red ring. As the ship got closer, I realized with a bolt of hope that I could see another ship. Had I really caught someone up?

As the Crosswind zoomed closer, I could see the other ship wasn't moving. It was the Zephyr, and one of its bridges was drowning in giant red and green shellfish.

As we whizzed past, I saw a massive fist fly up out of

the sea of snapping claws, and crabs and lobster-scorpion-things went flying through the air. I felt a stab of pity for the giant, natural instinct making me want to stop and help before the man was hurt.

But my goal was to stay alive, and it wasn't like there was anything I could really do to improve his situation.

We sped on, and I kept my eyes wide and alert, ready for the next jets to erupt from the ocean. Nothing came, though. The surface of the sea was deceptively calm, the sky clear and bright, drifting with coral-colored clouds.

We soared through the ring with no problem, and new inky lines spread across the beautiful sails, filling in more of the map. It could have been the bottom third of an island. I tried to remember the map of Olympus, to see if it was Sagittarius. Surely we wouldn't be going too far from where we had started?

I felt the ship slow down, and I frowned in alarm.

Shit. I didn't know where to go. That was the next hurdle, I realized. Looking left and right, I tried to make out any sign of ships in the distance. All I could see was the green of Sagittarius on my right, and the wide-open ocean on my left.

Shrugging, I steered the ship left. These were the Poseidon Trials after all, so the ocean was as good a call as any.

I risked taking my hands from the wheel, darting to the railings to look over. Nothing but bright blue sea, frothy waves dancing across the surface. I moved back to the wheel and kept my guard up, looking for any signs of rings.

I was just starting to worry that I'd gone in the wrong direction when pain lanced through my entire body. Kryvo began squealing and I whirled, trying to work out what was happening. The whole ship vibrated, and Atlas's warning came back to me: *If you leave the bounds of the race, you'll be alerted.*

I barely had the sentience to steer the ship in the opposite direction, the pressure in my skull was so bad. As soon as we started back toward the island though, the pain lessened, and eventually faded.

"You okay, Kryvo?"

"N-n-n-o."

"I'm sorry."

"This is a very stressful morning." His voice was tiny, and I felt bad for putting him through this. In an effort to make him feel better, or at least distract him, I pointed to the sail.

"Any ideas on that map?"

"I'll have a look," he said shakily.

"Thank you."

I didn't know how much time I'd lost sailing out in the wrong direction, but coming last wasn't really an issue, so I tried not to let it bother me. Keeping my eyes peeled for red rings, I willed the ship to soar over the ocean. My eyes caught on a dark patch of sky toward the north of Sagittarius. It stood out from the rest of the bright vista, and I angled the ship toward it. It was a storm, I realized as we got closer. A small, isolated storm that was churning a chunk of the ocean up into a heaving, roiling mass of power.

But sparking and catching the light every now and then, were flashes of red. The rings.

With a near debilitating bout of trepidation, I commanded the ship to fly into the storm.

CHAPTER 27

*a*s soon as the ship moved into the rain, I knew I was in trouble. Wind as strong as a battering ram slammed into the hull, and the vessel lurched.

"Almi?" Kryvo's unsure voice was barely audible over the sound of the rain pelting the deck. "This is not good!"

"We'll just get through the rings and get out of here!" I called back. But I could barely steer the ship, the rain and the wind were so powerful. The sea was half frigging whirlpool below me, it was so wild. I wanted to will the ship higher, in order to keep clear of the turbulent waves, but the rings were dangerously close to the surface.

Of course they were, I thought, snarling.

I couldn't keep the rain from lashing my face, making it hard to see without constantly wiping the water out of my eyes.

What felt like painfully slowly, we made our way closer to the first ring. The bottom of the hoop was practically skimming the churning waves.

"Nearly there!" I called to Kryvo, as much for my own encouragement as his.

I blinked through the hammering rain as a flash of lightning lit up my surroundings. There, in front of me and moving through the farthest ring, was a ship. A ship with a metal hull.

Was it Poseidon or Kalypso?

Either way, I couldn't believe I'd caught one of them up. The two Whirlwinds started the race first.

Spurred on by the revelation that I possibly wasn't as shit as I thought I was, I guided the ship through the first ring. Something thudded against the hull, and we rocked to the side.

"What was that?" Kryvo's terrified squeak reached me.

"I don't know, and I don't want to."

I tried to get the ship to rise, to put some distance between us and the surface of the sea before we got to the next ring, which was easily another half mile away, but it was getting so hard to control. It was as though the storm was quicksand, and it was taking all my concentration to get the Crosswind to move through it. The second I got distracted by something, the ship slowed to a crawl, dropping slowly back toward the water.

The thudding against the hull sounded again, and I begged the ship to move higher over the sea.

"Come on! You fly, and you fly so well! Up you go!"

My urgent bidding seemed to work, and we lifted higher, the pull of the sea lessening.

I gave a small sigh of relief as we moved more freely toward the next ring, but my relief was short lived. We had risen high enough that I could see what was leaping out of the waves below us, and my stomach clenched.

Rotbloods. That's what had been butting the side of the ship. Their evil eyes fixed on the ship as they dove in and out of the water, snapping their huge jaws. At least three of them were visible in the waves, keeping pace with us.

"Oh shit. We do not want to risk being near the water for long."

More rain lashed down, and I was starting to feel cold. My hands were numb around the spokes of the wheel, and my teeth were chattering as I swore aloud.

Reluctantly, I willed the ship lower as we approached the next ring. The thudding started instantly. As the sharks battered the sides of the hull, frenzied wind pulled at the sail, forcing me to give everything I had to keeping the ship steady with my mind.

With a surge, the rain thickened, a torrent of water gushing down over us as we moved through the gleaming red ring, barely visible in the storm now.

More lightning lit the horizon, and I looked out for the Whirlwind, but I couldn't even see the next ring any more.

Fearful of losing my bearings and flying through one we'd already completed, I wiped my face angrily, wishing my eyesight was better.

"Kryvo! Do you know where the next ring is?"

"No!"

A flash of blue and gold caught my eye in the gray, and I locked onto it. "Blue!"

The rain was lashing the pegasus as his wings beat

wildly. His eyes locked on mine and I knew instantly that he couldn't stay in the storm long. He turned in the air and flew fast.

"Follow Blue!" I commanded the ship.

My burst of grateful energy must have poured into the ship, because this time it was easier to rise from the magnet-like waves and force our way through the storm.

When the last ring came into view, I was numb from the cold. The final hoop was actually touching the surface of the sea, the angry waves sloshing over the curved bottom. The red of the rotbloods flashed and I saw that they were jumping through the hoop themselves, almost in a mockery of our task.

Screwing my face up, I willed the ship lower, aiming for the ring.

I expected the hammering of the rotbloods against the ship but there was nothing. As we dipped I lost sight of the sea beneath us, and focused on the glowing ring through the rain.

A furious gust of wind slammed into the ship, and the sail billowed out, dragging us off course. The whole ship tipped alarmingly, and I dug deep, desperately trying to keep her upright.

I watched almost in slow motion as we rocked the other way, and a wave came crashing toward us, higher than the hull. It was too late to veer out of the way, and besides—we'd reached the ring.

"Hang on Kryvo," I yelled, as the wave crashed over the deck.

The water was icy cold as it doused me head to foot, trying to rip me from the wheel. I gasped for breath as the wave drained away, my concentration severed, and the ship slowing. Another gust of vicious wind took us, and we rocked hard. I barely had time to see the mast tipping toward the edge of the red ring before a second wave crested over us. The power behind the second wave was so great it dragged the whole ship over, low enough for me to see the waiting forms of the demon sharks. That's why they weren't battering the ship. They didn't need to. They were waiting for me to be washed off the deck and into the deadly ocean.

And they were about to get their wish.

I was vaguely aware of the top of the mast snagging on the ring, and then I was thrown from the wheel as another wave slammed into the Crosswind.

My numb fingers screamed in protest as they were prized from the spokes, and I didn't have time to cry out before I was rolling down the now vertical deck. I slammed into the railings, and for a second, I thought I might be saved, but then freezing water rose up around me, and I realized the railings were sinking. The ship was capsizing.

CHAPTER 28

I tried to get to my feet on the sideways railings, but the lashing rain made getting a purchase on anything impossible.

"Kryvo!" I screamed, but I was too far from him to hear anything, and the wind was howling.

Flashes of red caught my eye, and I knew it wasn't the ring. I scrambled along the railing as it sank, trying to pull myself up the deck but it was impossibly sheer. If I didn't get out of the way, I'd be dragged fully under the ship. But throwing myself into the ocean with the sharks was as sure a death as drowning.

Control the ship!

Poseidon's voice bellowed into my mind, so loud it hurt.

Control the ship? Could I will it to obey me like this?

Gripping the wooden slats of the rails I begged the vessel to rise.

"Up! Go up! Take the fucking ring with you if it's stuck!" I screamed at the ship.

A wave crashed over my head, submerging me completely, and I clung to the rails as my body was lifted from them. The deck was vertical behind me, trapping me, and I saw the rotbloods speeding through the water toward me.

I had less than a second before it reached me.

The water swirled between me and the shark and then Poseidon was there, his back to me and facing the predator. He raised a spear and launched it at the shark. Turning, he moved through the water like lightning, his eyes electric blue in the gray water. He grabbed my arm, pulling me from the railing as a current of water began to push us from beneath. We burst through the surface together, riding the wave as though it were some sort of surfboard. Pulling me tight against his body we continued to fly through the air, and over his shoulder I could see a second wave rise up under the Crosswind and lift it from the ocean. With a surge, it was wrenched free from the hoop, and then it was speeding after us on its own wave. We broke through the edge of the storm and I gasped for breath as the rain vanished, bright pastel skies calm above us.

The wave we were riding swerved, depositing us on the deck of the now righted Crosswind.

Poseidon moved, gripping my shoulders and holding me at arm's length, checking every inch of my body.

"Th-th-thanks," I gasped. I was so cold I could hardly move my limbs, and I was pretty sure shock was setting in.

"You nearly died," Poseidon growled. I'd never seen his eyes so wild, a vivid version of the storm he had just rescued me from. I stared up at him. Warmth was starting to seep into me from where he was gripping me, and now we were out of the storm I could feel my strength slowly returning.

"You saved me. Again."

"Almi." Emotion was choking his words and I blinked at him. He looked every inch a god, fierce and solid and oozing blinding, lethal power. Yet at the same time, he looked utterly helpless. "I will always save you."

Before I could even process his words he pulled me to him, taking my lips with his. Desire exploded through me as he kissed me like a man with nothing to lose, a man starved. A man who had never wanted anything so much.

And I kissed him back, my own ferocity matching his. I pressed myself against him, desperate to feel every part of his body, for him to be as close to me as was physically possible.

He was right. Right in every way, and I didn't know how I'd ever not known this feeling was possible.

With a wrench he stepped back, breaking the kiss. My lips tingled, and I gaped at him, flushed and dizzy, desire pounding through my body and pooling between my legs in the most alien and incredible, way.

"No, this can't... I thought I was going to lose you. I'm sorry. I'm sorry, Almi."

"Wait—!" But I was too late. With a flash of white light, he was gone.

"What the fuck!"

The expletive burst from my lips, and I lifted my hands to my head in frustration, my limbs shaking.

A squeak caught my attention, and I looked at the bridge. "Shit, Kryvo!"

I took the steps two at a time, astounded I had the energy to do so, and saw the red starfish still clinging to the wheel.

"Kryvo, jeez, I'm sorry."

"W-w-w-e s-s-survived?"

"We did. Poseidon saved us." I shook my head. "Then he kissed me like I was his actual wife and he'd never wanted anyone so much in his life, and then he fucked off."

The starfish paused in his shivering. "He did?"

"Yeah."

I slumped down to the planks, needing a second to sit.

"Are we still in the race?"

"Yes. But we nearly drowned and got eaten." *And was kissed by a man I thought I hated and who hated me.* "I don't care if we come last. I need a moment."

I heard the sound of wings beating, then Blue landed on the bridge beside me. He tossed his mane as I looked up at him. "Hey, Blue. Thanks for your help in there."

He whinnied.

"Do you get whiplash from Poseidon's mood swings?" I asked the pegasus.

He stamped his feet.

"Yeah, maybe just me. That man is complicated."

I didn't know what it said about me that I seemed to be more shaken by the kiss than the ship capsizing in the storm and delivering me to the rotbloods.

"We should get this over with," I said, trying to pull myself together. I was distinctly aware that I was avoiding bringing Lily's image into my mind, almost as though I wasn't ready for her opinion on what had just happened. I needed my emotions to stay private, to belong to just me, a little longer. Just until I could make sense of them. And I couldn't do that out here, knowing I had to survive this stupid trial.

I stood up, dragging my shaking, confused ass up off the planks. Need was still pulsing through me, and I could feel the god's presence on my lips, his wild gaze burned into my brain.

I shook my head, clenching my jaw hard.

"Later," I told myself aloud. "Deal with this later. Right now, you need to focus."

I looked around me at the clear skies. Blue stamped his hooves and snorted.

"You know where we're going next, Blue?"

He ran a few steps along the planks, then launched himself into the air, his gold wings stunning in the light. "Follow the pegasus," I told the ship, as I retook my position at the wheel, trying to lock my spiraling thoughts about Poseidon away where they couldn't distract me from the lethal task at hand.

CHAPTER 29

*A*fter a couple of minutes, we were flying over the west coast of Sagittarius, a mountain range consisting of only three mountains to my right. But boy were they big. Conjoined lower down, they spread out like a huge ridge on the landscape, and I would have expected them to be covered in snow in the human world, but here they were covered in a sheet of green.

Blue dipped ahead of us, and I commanded the ship to move lower, and increase her speed as we chased after him. She responded immediately, and the wind stung my eyes as we went faster. Sailing over land didn't have the same feeling, the same scents or openness, that sailing over the water did.

The pegasus made a sudden dive, his golden wings catching the light of the sky as he dropped from view.

I let go of the wheel and moved to the railing, the ship slowing down as I did so. There was Blue, kicking his hooves in the sand on the beach below us. Nestled in the sand also were three massive treasure chests, separated by tall palm trees. A sense of trepidation filled me at the quiet calm of the scene below.

"Have I gotta go down to the beach, Blue?" I called as the ship came to a gentle stop.

I couldn't hear the Pegasus, but he flicked his head, mane waving, and stamped on the sand.

"Oh boy." I really, really didn't want to get off the ship. But if that's what the Trial called for, then that's what I would have to do. "Let's go, Kryvo," I said, picking up the little starfish.

"I'd rather stay here," he squeaked.

I lifted him to my face. "What if I need your help?"

He gave a rippling squeaky noise that I thought was his equivalent of a sigh. "I shall accompany you," he said reluctantly.

"Thanks, buddy."

I set him on my collarbone and headed for the hauler at the back of the bridge. I stepped into the rickety wooden crate, pulled the shutter across it and willed it to lower. It did so immediately.

The sand was a few feet below me when it stopped moving, the Crosswind hovering a person's height above the ground and the hauler dropping just lower than its hull.

Carefully, I jumped down. The powdery-soft sand took the thump out of my landing, and I straightened. Blue trotted toward me, then turned pointedly to face the chests.

Now I was down here, they looked even larger. They also looked deliberately placed, palm trees between them, and large rocky boulders poking out of what looked like jungle behind them. Wind blew across my face, carrying the scent of the sea, and I turned instinctively to check for demon crabs or sharks or anything else crawling out of the water to eat me.

There was nothing but gentle waves lapping at the sandy shore.

I turned back to the enormous treasure chests and walked cautiously toward one. My foot hit something hard in the sand, and I looked down.

Bone. It was a long bone, picked clean and gleaming ivory.

"Huh. Please don't let that belong to any of the other contestants," I muttered. "Except maybe Ceto."

"I'm not sure she even has bones," said Kryvo.

I glanced up at the sky, checking for other ships, though I was positive that I was well behind everyone else after the storm. Unless, of course, Polybotes never escaped the crabs.

Blue whinnied, drawing my gaze back down.

I steeled myself and moved purposefully toward the first chest, eying it warily.

It was almost as tall as I was and made of a rich, shining wood. It didn't appear to have any age to it at all. When I moved, the light caught on the wood, and I saw a faint greeny-blue shimmer. Iron bands lined the rounded top, and it looked for all the world like it could have come from the set of a pirate movie.

Except for where the padlock should have been. There, there was just a shining bronze plate with one word etched into it. "Stingray."

I frowned, then moved backward, careful not to touch

anything. The second one shimmered red in the light, and the plate on the front said 'Seagrass'. The last chest shimmered purple and had 'Seashell' written on it.

"Right," I said out loud, chewing on my lip as I clasped my chin. "What the fuck are we supposed to do now?"

"Is there anything else here?" squeaked Kryvo.

I turned in a slow circle, eyes sharp.

"Yes!" There, pinned on a palm tree, was a sheet of paper, its slight fluttering in the breeze catching my attention. I hurried over to it, tearing it from the pin.

See here before you, chests numbering three
  Each is different, and only one will set you free
  All the other two hold is certain death
  Get it wrong and you will draw your last breath
  Rage and fire lie within the wrong box
  Avoid your body burning on the rocks
  Select with care the chest that holds no doom
  Surely that will keep you from an early tomb

I blinked as I read the words, then read them aloud for Kryvo.

"So, we have to open one of the chests?"

"Yes. The one that won't kill us."

"And... How the hell are we supposed to know which one that is?"

The starfish made his sighing noise again. "We can work this out. It says each is different, right?"

I nodded. "Yup."

"What's different about them?"

"They all shimmer a different color, and they have different words written on them. Seashell, stingray and seagrass."

I peered at the riddle in my hands, looking for something I'd missed.

"Rage and fire. That sounds…"

"Like something we want to avoid at all costs?" offered Kryvo.

"Yeah." A slight panic was starting to make me twitchy. This wasn't something we could walk away from. There was a one in three chance we would get this wrong, and die. And unlike the geysers and the storm, I couldn't just strap on my big girl pants and fly straight into it, hoping for the best. This challenge gave me time to think, time to question. Time for fear to settle in.

"Read it one more time," said Kryvo.

I did, staring at the words, willing them to give us more.

"I like seashells," I said, unhelpfully.

"I like stingrays," the starfish responded, equally unhelpfully.

I blew out a breath, looking again between the three chests. I used to do puzzles on my phone when I was bored in my trailer. Surely I could work this one out?

"Maybe it's a word game," I murmured, looking back at the riddle, trying something new.

See here before you, chests numbering three
Each is different and only one will set you free

All the other two hold is certain death
Get it wrong, and you will draw your last breath
Rage and fire lie within the wrong box
Avoid your body burning on the rocks
Select with care the chest that holds no doom
Surely that will keep you from an early tomb

I saw it in an instant, letting out a whoop of triumph.

Kryvo squeaked in surprise.

"Don't do that!" he admonished.

"But Kryvo, look!" I held up the paper. "It *is* a word game. Look at the first letter of each line!"

The starfish slowly read out each letter. "It spells seagrass."

Grinning like an idiot, I strode toward the chest that had the plate that read seagrass. "Who needs saving now?" I beamed.

I laid my hand on the chest, and looked around, unsure how to make my selection. "This one," I said loudly. I had no idea if that was how I was supposed to do it, but it was worth a try.

There was a loud clicking sound, and painfully slowly, the chest creaked open. Just when I thought nothing was going to happen, red sparks flew into the air, rushing from the open chest. They danced in the sky a moment, then zoomed higher, forming three large hoops.

"Yes!" I turned to Blue, grinning, and a loud rumble sounded. The pegasus neighed, then took flight, wings beating hard to make up for his lack of run up.

A heartbeat later I wished I could fly too.

The sand beneath my feet was moving. Sinking.

"Shit." I ran, powering my arms and willing my legs to be strong. Every step felt like I was fighting a battle though, the sand trying to suck my body down. I threw a glance over my shoulder, fear pounding through me as I saw the chests were half submerged in the quicksand.

I'd begun moving just early enough that my momentum was carrying me, but my ship seemed a frigging mile away as the suck of the sand increased.

Blue swooped down in front of me, flicking his tail, and I didn't question his intention.

I reached out and grabbed it and he beat his wings, his strength helping to move me faster across the sand.

"You're a fucking legend, Blue!" I yelled at him, furiously working my legs as we closed in on the hauler dangling from the back of the Crosswind. With a desperate leap, I let go of Blue's tail and threw myself into the crate. Landing hard on my shoulder, I heard the snapping of wood and thought the bottom might give out under my weight. Breath held, I waited to fall into the deadly sand below.

"Almi?" squeaked Kryvo when nothing happened. "P-p-p-p-please take us up to the bridge."

"Good plan," I said exhaling hard, my heart pounding so fast I thought it might escape my ribcage. "I'm not built to run that fast."

I felt sick as I willed the hauler to take us up, but my nausea was fast replaced by relief when I stepped shakily out onto the sturdy planks of the ship.

I moved to the ship's wheel and closed my fingers around the spokes, feeling my hands shake a little less at the now familiar warmth the ship gave me. "Take us through the rings, please," I whispered to the ship. We swung around as we rose, then she sailed through the gleaming rings, one by one. I was tense as we flew, waiting for the next curveball to come our way, but it appeared that the quicksand had been deemed enough of a challenge for the time being. We were unhindered as we passed through the rings.

I watched the spidery ink on the solar sails spread out further, tilting my head as the last three sections of the map appeared, then coalesced into something readable.

"Any ideas Kryvo?"

"Yes. You see those three shapes around the cross?"

I looked at the map as the sail snapped taut, as though it was trying to help me. The map looked like someone had zoomed in very close to a single part of Olympus, and there was a giant cross in the middle of three roughly round shapes. Something moved under the cross, the ink swirling across the glittering fabric of the sail.

"Yes."

"I believe those are three small volcanoes on the other side of Aquarius, the north-easterly part of Scorpio."

"Yeah?"

"Do you want me to show you the map of Olympus I am seeing in the palace through my starfish friends?"

I shook my head. "No, I trust you." Blue had been with us too long now to have seen where anyone had gone before us, so I assumed he couldn't help us. But the little starfish had got everything right so far, and I had no reason to hold us up any longer.

I willed the ship to move west. The ink moved again

on the map, as though it were zooming in further on the cross. Did that mean we were going in the right direction?

Whatever kept moving under the cross was getting larger.

The further we flew, the more the cool gusts of ocean air calmed my fried nerves. I refused to let myself think about the kiss or anything else Poseidon-related, just focusing on getting to our destination. A couple of times the map started to zoom out instead of in, until I adjusted our course. The closer to the cross we got though, the more the thing under it came into focus.

It was a skull, I realized, once most of the map was dominated by the cross and the three representations of the volcanos.

"What do you think the skull means?"

Kryvo chittered. "What do you *think* it means? There's something there that will try to kill us."

CHAPTER 30

*J*ust a few moments later, shining in the distance, we saw the finish-line. It was a long shining line made of the same sparks as all the hoops were, the tips of three volcanoes visible in the distance.

Squinting, I could make out three small dots hovering the other side of the red line. Ships that had already finished the race, I presumed. And there were only three, which meant someone was behind me. *Or dead.* I found myself willing one of the ships on the other side to be Poseidon's Whirlwind.

I resisted the urge to propel the Crosswind forward, taking my time to scan the sea below me for any sign whatever Kryvo believed might be stalking these waters. I was in no rush. And frankly, I was astonished not to be last.

Though I wouldn't even have survived if it weren't for Poseidon's interventions. *Again.*

"I need to learn to rescue my own damned ass," I muttered.

"Or hide."

I rolled my eyes at the starfish. A deep growling sound reached my ears, and Blue swooped above us.

"What was that?" Kryvo asked hesitantly.

I willed the ship to move a bit higher, and a bit faster. "I don't know," I answered, as the growl grew louder. Thunder clapped suddenly, and then something burst up from the water before us. Wooden planks, I realized, as I swerved the Crosswind instinctively.

My mouth fell open as I watched the shattered pieces of a ship shower up in an arc before us, before falling back down to the waves below.

"Oh my god," I breathed, trying to resist the urge to run and look over the edge of the ship. "Whose ship was destroyed?"

"And by what?" Kryvo's voice was wobbly with fear, and I jumped in fright as Blue's hooves landed noisily on the deck.

I turned to him and saw that he was skittering his feet uneasily, shaking his head and snorting continuously.

A deep sense of unease gripped me.

"What's wrong, Blue?" He whinnied loudly, the sound pained.

I couldn't tell how I knew what he was trying to tell me, but I did.

Poseidon. It's Poseidon's ship.

Letting go of the wheel, I ran to the edge of the railings and looked over.

. . .

Just a few feet below the crystal-clear water was the god of the sea. And wrapped around him was the tail of something that looked like it had come straight out of a Jurassic Park film.

Terror made my muscles freeze, and I watched in horror as Poseidon was lifted clear above the surface of the sea, then slammed back down with a force that would have killed a human.

The creature was larger than my ship, and shaped like a crocodile at its bottom half, its barbed tail wrapped tight around Poseidon. Its top half was dinosaur-like, its long reptilian snout filled with enormous teeth, and its beady eyes fiercely intelligent. Six arms like crabs' legs, jointed and ending in fierce looking spikes, jutted out of its body, flailing toward Poseidon, and blue tendrils that almost looked like feathers lined its neck and back, glowing.

"What do we do?" I half-shrieked, digging in my pouches.

I threw in a grenade, watching as it gave a little poof and sent ink spreading through the water utterly ineffectually.

Blue galloped to my side, shaking his mane and neighing. I looked at the Pegasus, my mind racing.

The finish line was a hundred meters away. The monster guarding it was not at all interested in me. I knew what I was supposed to do.

The monster lifted Poseidon again, this time pulling him into his torso, the spiked arms bending in to stab at him. Light blasted from Poseidon's body, blasting back the spikes, but only for a moment.

With an agonizing screech, the creature moved faster

than I thought it would be able to, rushing through the ocean. I lost sight of it as it moved under the ship, and I ran to the other side of the ship just as it leapt out of the water. It arched high as it jumped, a grotesque parody of dolphins playing, its prey clutched in its tail.

My heart thudded, my chest constricting, as I saw Poseidon's face. Half of it was the color of granite.

"No," I whispered, fear coiling in my gut inexplicably. Poseidon's eyes met mine for a fraction of a second, before he was dragged back under the surface.

I leaned over, looking for them under the water. There was an almighty splash and then Poseidon's voice rang through the air.

"Go back to the depths you came from!"

And then he was there, three times his normal size, fierce and strong and unstoppable, a tidal wave lifting him from the ocean as a whirlpool of water formed before his towering form. The creature thrashed and flailed in the churning water, and Poseidon raised both his hands, his eyes closing.

Glowing such an intense turquoise that I could barely see, he roared. The light rushed the monster, and it spasmed as the magic flooded its body. With a jerk, it exploded in a mass of light and scales.

Relief rushed from me, my whole body sagging against the rails. "Thank fuck for that."

Poseidon turned on his wave, his eyes locking on mine, and all my relief vanished.

The light was leaving his body, replaced entirely by stone. Horror took me as sadness filled his expression, before the light left his eyes. Slowly, terrifyingly slowly, his stone form tipped and fell from the collapsing wave.

"Poseidon!" I screamed his name as I watched his granite form sink below the surface.

A hundred emotions rushed me. Lily's face filled my mind. I felt myself reach for the frantic pegasus beside me.

"I'm sorry, Lily," I half sobbed, as I pulled myself clumsily onto the winged horse's back. "I'm sorry, I have to. I don't know why." All I knew was that I couldn't let him sink to the bottom of the sea.

I had to save him.

Go.

A gust of ocean wind lifted me as Blue snapped his wings out and sprang into the air.

I had time for one big breath before we dove into the ocean after Poseidon.

THANKS FOR READING!

Thank you so much for reading! If you enjoyed the first book of Almi and Poseidon's story, I would be so grateful for a review.

You can find the next book, Surrender of the Brutal King, on Amazon.

You can get exclusive access to cut scenes and first looks at artwork and story ideas, plus free short stories and audiobooks if you sign up to my newsletter at elizaraine.com and you can hang out with me and get teasers, giveaways and release updates (and pictures of my pets) by joining my Facebook reader group, just search for Eliza Raine Author!

Printed in Great Britain
by Amazon

29290787R00130